SEA STORIES

SEA STORIES

A CLASSIC ILLUSTRATED EDITION

Compiled by Cooper Edens

chronicle books · san francisco

To the memory of Cecil the Seasick Sea Serpent
and Captain Huff 'n' Puff —*C. E.*

The publisher gratefully acknowledges permission to reprint excerpts from the following works:

"Octopus's Garden," by Richard Starkey © 1969. Courtesy of Startling Music Ltd.

"Puff the Magic Dragon," by Peter Yarrow and Leonard Lipton © 1963. Copyright renewed 1991 by
Silver Dawn Music. Courtesy of Pepamar Music.

"When the Ship Comes In," by Bob Dylan © 1963. Courtesy of Warner Bros Inc.

The Old Man and the Sea, by Ernest Hemingway © 1952. Copyright renewed 1968 by
Muriel Hemingway. Courtesy of Seawest Inc.

Little Toot, by Hardie Gramatky © 1939. Excerpt of text and illustration reproduced by
permission of The Putnam & Grosset Group, New York.

"Jamaica Farewell," by Erving Burgess © 1955. Courtesy of Shari Music Pub. Corp.

"Under the Boardwalk," by Arthur Resnick and Kenny Young © 1964. Courtesy of Hudson Bay Music Co.

Peter Pan, by Sir J. M. Barrie © 1904. Copyright renewed 1995 by
Great Ormond Street Hospital Children's Charity. Courtesy of Great Ormond Street Hospital for Children.

Book design by Susan Van Horn.
Typeset in Minion and Bernhard Modern.
Manufactured in China.

Library of Congress Cataloging-in-Publication Data
Sea stories : a classic illustrated edition / compiled by Cooper Edens.
p. cm.
Summary: A collection of poems, stories, historical essays, fairy tales,
and myths related to the sea, including tales of pirates, mermaids, Vikings,
and sea monsters, illustrated by well-known artists.
ISBN-13: 978-0-8118-5634-8
ISBN-10: 0-8118-5634-8
1. Ocean—Literary collections. [1. Ocean—Literary collections.
2. Sea stories.] I. Edens, Cooper.
PZ5.S4365 2007
[Fic]—dc22
2006013301

Distributed in Canada by Raincoast Books
9050 Shaughnessy Street, Vancouver, British Columbia V6P 6E5

10 9 8 7 6 5 4 3 2 1

Chronicle Books LLC
680 Second Street, San Francisco, California 94107

www.chroniclekids.com

Preface

Dear Reader, forgive my indulgence, but I've always wished myself part of the *Nautilus* crew:

COOPER EDENS: You love the sea, don't you, Captain Nemo?

CAPTAIN NEMO: *"Yes, I love it! The sea is everything. It covers seven-tenths of the globe. Its breath is pure and healthy. It is an immense universe where man is never alone, for he can feel life quivering all about him. The sea is only a receptacle for all the prodigious, supernatural things that exist inside it; it is only movement and love; it is the living infinite. And in fact it is made up of the three kingdoms of nature—mineral, vegetable, and animal. The sea is a vast reservoir of nature. The world, so to speak, began with the sea, and who knows but that it will also end in the sea! There lies supreme tranquility."*

The sea is indeed impressive, and to this list of the sea's virtues, let me add the great authors and illustrators who have written of and portrayed the wonders of the sea. Jules Verne, Robert Louis Stevenson, Lewis Carroll, Herman Melville, Daniel Defoe, Sir J. M. Barrie, Rudyard Kipling, Ernest Hemingway, Jessie Willcox Smith, Margaret Tarrant, the Robinson Brothers, Charles and Heath, Maxfield Parrish, and Maria Kirk have all expressed in their work their great love for the sea.

I am pleased to have brought all this ocean treasure together, and hope the reader will find it as varied, as beautiful, and as fascinating as the sea. Now, Captain Nemo, if you will allow me, I would like to look over the *Nautilus*.

—*Cooper Edens*

Contents

The Legend of Atlantis

*This tantalizing legend has had many tellings—
and many believers and disbelievers.*

The first mention of the island of Atlantis appeared during the 300s B.C. in two works by the Greek philosopher Plato. Plato told the story of a brilliant civilization that once existed on Atlantis. But according to legend, the island and its people sank mysteriously into the sea, and were never seen again.

Plato's tales of Atlantis fascinated many people of later times. Various theories about the location of the island and how it disappeared have been proposed, and a number of expeditions have attempted to discover the ruins of Atlantis. Most scientists think that the Greek island of Thera, which disappeared almost completely during a volcanic eruption, may have been the historical basis for the legend. Other people think Atlantis was an entire continent that lay between Europe and North America. Whatever the truth, the legend of Atlantis continues to fascinate people with the idea of a land lost at the bottom of the sea.

The Walrus and the Carpenter

(An excerpt)

BY LEWIS CARROLL

The sun was shining on the sea,
Shining with all his might:
He did his best to make
The billows smooth and bright—
And this was odd, because it was
The middle of the night.

The moon was shining sulkily,
Because she thought the sun
Had got no business to be there
After the day was done—
"It's very rude of him," she said,
"To come and spoil the fun!"

The Walrus and the Carpenter
Were walking close at hand;
They wept like anything to see
Such quantities of sand:
"If this were only cleared away,"
They said, "It would be grand!"

"O Oysters, come and walk with us!"
The Walrus did beseech.
"A pleasant walk, a pleasant talk,
Along the briny beach:
We cannot do with more than four,
To give a hand to each."

The eldest Oyster looked at him,
But never a word he said:
The eldest Oyster winked his eye,
And shook his heavy head—
Meaning to say he did not choose
To leave the oyster bed.

But four young Oysters hurried up,
All eager for the treat:
Their coats were brushed, their faces
washed,
Their shoes were clean and neat—
And this was odd, because, you know,
They hadn't any feet.

Four other Oysters followed them,
And yet another four;
And thick and fast they came at last,
And more, and more, and more—
All hopping through the frothy waves,
And scrambling to the shore.

The Walrus and the Carpenter
Walked on a mile or so,
And then they rested on a rock
Conveniently low:
And all the little Oysters stood
And waited in a row.

"The time has come," the Walrus said,
"To talk of many things:
Of shoes—and ships—and sealing wax—
Of cabbages—and kings—
And why the sea is boiling hot—
And whether pigs have wings."

"But wait a bit," the Oysters cried,
"Before we have our chat;
For some of us are out of breath,
And all of us are fat!"
"No hurry!" said the Carpenter.
They thanked him much for that.

"A loaf of bread," the Walrus said,
"Is what we chiefly need:
Pepper and vinegar besides
Are very good indeed—
Now if you're ready, Oysters dear,
We can begin to feed."

"But not on us!" the Oysters cried,
Turning a little blue.
"After such kindness, that would be
A dismal thing to do!"
"The night is fine," the Walrus said,
"Do you admire the view?

"It was so kind of you to come!
And you are very nice!"
The Carpenter said nothing but
"Cut us another slice:
I wish you were not quite so deaf—
I've had to ask you twice!"

"It seems a shame," the Walrus said,
"To play them such a trick,
After we've brought them out so far,
And made them trot so quick!"
The Carpenter said nothing but
"The butter's spread too thick!"

"I weep for you," the Walrus said:
"I deeply sympathize."
With sobs of tears he sorted out
Those of the largest size,
Holding his pocket handkerchief
Before his streaming eyes.

"O Oysters," said the Carpenter,
"You've had a pleasant run!
Shall we be trotting home again?"
But answer came there none—
And this was scarcely odd, because
They'd eaten every one.

Blackbeard the Pirate

Edward Teach, alias Blackbeard, was one of the wildest villains in the pirate business. So many tales are told about him, it is hard to sift out the facts, but here I've done my best. What is clear is that he frightened people a great deal.

Edward Teach was known as Blackbeard because his jet-black beard almost completely covered his face, even going around his eyes. He made the most of his fierce looks, twisting the ends of his hair into small pigtails and turning them around his ears. He would place hemp cord under his pirate hat, then set the ends on fire. When he confronted enemies, the lighted tapers in his hair belched out smoke as they burned, scaring his victims out of their wits. He wore six pistols strapped across his chest and glared at his prisoners so madly that they believed he was the devil himself.

Blackbeard was born in England around 1680 and as a young man began his career as a privateer (a kind of legal pirate). His first captain, Benjamin Hornigold, was impressed by Blackbeard, who didn't waste time waiting for victims to take their rings off—he just chopped off their fingers and dropped them in his pocket. When the privateers eventually captured a sloop, Blackbeard was made captain.

Building up a squadron of four or five ships, Blackbeard worked along the coast of the Carolinas. Once, within a few days, he captured five ships off of Charleston, terrifying the city's inhabitants. The merchant ships in the harbor were so scared of the notorious Blackbeard that they refused to leave anchorage, and all commerce was suspended.

One incident illustrates Blackbeard's insane behavior. While drinking in the ship's cabin with a friend one evening, he suddenly pulled out a pistol. Holding it under the table, Blackbeard shot the man in the knee, crippling him for life. "Why did you injure your friend?" he was later asked by a crewmember. "If I do not," Blackbeard is said to have replied, "you'll forget who I am."

Planters and merchants who had suffered great losses from Blackbeard's raids finally got fed up. Knowing how corrupt North Carolina's governor was, they appealed to Governor Spotswood of Virginia for help. He sent out two armed sloops, crewed by the British navy, to capture Blackbeard's pirates.

The two forces met at Ocracoke Inlet, off the coast of North Carolina, in November of 1718. A broadside from Blackbeard's flagship, which had 40 guns, disabled one sloop. When the cannon smoke cleared, Blackbeard moved his ship alongside the other sloop and, with 14 of his men, jumped aboard. A bloody hand-to-hand struggle began, with sabers flashing and pistol shots exploding. Nearly every man was bathed in blood when the sloop's officer, Lt. Robert Maynard, came to grips with Blackbeard. The pirate chief kept firing his six pistols as sabers slashed him. Even with 20 saber cuts and five shots in him, Blackbeard continued fighting until one of Maynard's men, with a great swoop of his broadsword, cut off Blackbeard's head. When they saw they had lost their leader, the surviving pirates surrendered or jumped in the sea.

On Lt. Maynard's orders, the pirate's bearded head was suspended below the sloop's bowsprit. When that grisly trophy came into view at the harbor, the crowd roared its gratitude.

Peter Pan

(Mermaids' Lagoon passage)

BY SIR J. M. BARRIE

If you shut your eyes and are a lucky one, you may see at times a shapeless pool of lovely pale colors suspended in the darkness; then if you squeeze your eyes tighter, the pool begins to take shape, and the colors become so vivid that with another squeeze they must go on fire. But just before they go on fire you see the lagoon. This is the nearest you ever get to it on the mainland, just one heavenly moment; if there could be two moments you might see the surf and hear the mermaids singing.

The children often spent long summer days on this lagoon, swimming or floating most of the time, playing the mermaid games in the water, and so forth. You must not think from this that the mermaids were on friendly terms with them; on the contrary, it was among Wendy's lasting regrets that all the time she was on the island she never had a civil word from one of them. When she stole softly to the edge of the lagoon she might see them by the score, especially on Marooners' Rock, where they loved to bask, combing out their hair in a lazy way that quite irritated her; or she might even swim, on tiptoe as it were, to within a yard of them, but then they saw her and dived, probably splashing her with their tails, not by accident, but intentionally.

They treated all the boys in the same way, except of course Peter, who chatted with them on Marooners' Rock by the hour, and sat on their tails when they got cheeky. He gave Wendy one of their combs.

The most haunting time at which to see them is at the turn of the moon, when they utter strange wailing cries; but the lagoon is dangerous for mortals then, and until the evening of which we have now to tell, Wendy had never seen the lagoon by moonlight, less from fear, for of course Peter would have accompanied her, than because she had strict rules about every one being in bed by seven. She was often at the lagoon, however, on sunny days after rain, when the mermaids come up in extraordinary numbers to play with their bubbles. The bubbles of many colors made in rainbow water they treat as balls, hitting them gaily from one to another with their tails, and trying to keep them in the rainbow till they burst. The goals are at each end of the rainbow, and the keepers only are allowed to use their hands. Sometimes hundreds of mermaids will be playing in the lagoon at a time, and it is quite a pretty sight.

Sinbad the Sailor

This story is adapted from Andrew Lang's 1898 translation of 1,001 Arabian Nights, *which was written about 900* A.D. *At that time, stories about sailing were not as much about the sea as about the adventures to be found in faraway lands, as you'll find in this famous tale. In all, Sinbad went on seven voyages. This is his second.*

After my first voyage I decided to spend the rest of my days quietly in Baghdad; but, after a time, I grew weary of quiet life. My inclination to travel revived, and soon I put to sea a second time, with merchants of known probity. We traded from island to island, and exchanged commodities with great profit.

One day we landed on an island covered with several sorts of fruit trees, but we could see neither man nor beast upon it. We went to take a little fresh air in the meadows, and along the streams. While some diverted themselves in gathering fruits, I took wine and provisions and sat down by a stream. I made a good meal, and afterward fell asleep. I cannot tell how long I slept, but when I awoke the ship was gone.

I was very much surprised. I got up and looked about everywhere, but could not see even one of the merchants who landed with me. At last I perceived the ship under sail, but at such a distance that I lost sight of her in a very little time.

I was ready to die with grief. I cried out, beat my head and breast, and threw myself upon the ground, where I lay some time in terrible agony. I upbraided myself a hundred times for not being content with the profits of my first voyage, that might well have served me all my life. But all was in vain.

At last I resigned myself to the will of God, and not knowing what else to do, I climbed to the top of a great tree, whence I looked about on all sides to see if there was anything that could give me hope. When I looked toward the sea, I could see nothing but sky and water; but looking toward land I saw something white, and coming down I took up what provisions I had left and went toward it.

When I came nearer, I thought it to be a white bowl of a prodigious height and size; and when I came up to it I touched it, and found it to be very smooth. I went round to see if it was open on any side, but it was not, and there was no climbing up to the top of it as it was so smooth. It was at least fifty paces around.

By this time the sun was ready to set, and all of a sudden the sky became dark as if it had been covered with a thick cloud. I was astonished at this, but much more so when I found it occasioned by a bird of monstrous size that came flying toward me. I remembered a fowl, called a *roc*, that I had heard mariners speak of, and conceived that the great bowl I so much admired must in fact be its egg. The bird alighted and sat over the egg. As I perceived her coming, I crept close to the egg so that I had before me one of the legs of the bird, which was as big as the trunk of a tree. I tied myself securely to it with the cloth that went round my turban, in hopes that when the roc flew away she would carry me with her away from this desert island. After having passed the night in this position, the bird flew away next morning, as soon as it was day, and carried me so high that I could see the earth; she afterward descended all of a sudden, with such rapidity that I lost my senses; but when the roc was settled and I found myself on the ground I speedily untied the knot, and had scarce done so when the bird, having taken up a serpent of monstrous length in her bill, flew away.

The place where it left me was a deep valley, encompassed on all sides with mountains so high that they seemed to reach above the clouds, and so full of rocks that there was no possibility of getting out. This was a new perplexity; so that when I compared this place with the desert island, I found that I had gained nothing by the change.

As I walked through this valley, I perceived it was strewed with diamonds, some of a surprising size. I took great pleasure to look upon them; until finally I sat down upon one and, not having shut my eyes during the night, I fell asleep. But I had scarce shut my eyes when something fell by me with great noise and awoke me. This was a great piece of fresh meat; at the same time I saw several others fall down from the rocks in different places.

I always looked upon it to be a fable when I heard mariners and others discourse of the valley of diamonds, and of the stratagem made use of by merchants to get jewels thence, but now I found it to be true. Merchants come to the neighborhood of this valley and, throwing great joints of meat into the valley, wait for the giant eagles to dive down to pick the meat up. The diamonds stick in the meat and the merchants retrieve the diamonds from the eagles' nests.

I began to gather together the largest diamonds, and put them into the bag in which I used to carry my provisions. I afterward took the largest piece of meat I could find, tied it close around me, and lay on the ground with my face downward, the bag of diamonds tied fast to my belt.

I had scarce laid me down before the eagles came; each of them seized a piece of meat, and one of the strongest, having taken me up, carried me to his nest on top of the mountain. The merchants fell straightaway to shouting, to frighten the eagles; and when they had obliged them to quit their prey, one of them came to the nest where I was. He was very much afraid when he saw me; but, recovering himself, he began to quarrel with me, and asked why I stole his goods.

"You will treat me," replied I, "with more civility when you know me better. I have diamonds enough for you and myself too, more than all the merchants together." And having spoken these words, I showed them to him. I had scarce done speaking when the other merchants came trooping about, much astonished to see me.

They carried me to the place where they stayed, and there having opened my bag, were surprised at the largeness of my diamonds, and confessed that they never saw any that came near them. I prayed the merchant to whom the nest belonged whither I was carried (for every merchant had his own) to take as many as he pleased. He contented himself with one, and that too the least of them; and when I pressed him to take more, "No," said he. "I am well satisfied with this, which is valuable enough to save me the trouble of making any more voyages, to raise as great a fortune as I desire."

We left the place next morning and traveled across high mountains, where there were serpents of prodigious length, which we had the good fortune to escape. We took the first port we came to, and arrived at the isle of Roha, where the trees that yield camphor grow.

Here I exchanged some of my diamonds for good merchandise. From thence we went to other isles; and at last, we landed at Balsora, whence I went to Baghdad and lived honorably upon the riches I had gained with so much fatigue. There I gave sequins to the poor, and desired them to come and dine every day with me, that they might all their days have reason to remember Sinbad the sailor.

The Loch Ness Monster

Many people have claimed to have glimpsed this animal in the mysterious waters of Loch Ness, and a very blurry photograph—supposedly of the monster—was taken in 1933. Tourists have been journeying to Loch Ness ever since.

The Loch Ness Monster is a large, legendary animal that some people believe lives in Loch Ness, an inland sea (long ago connected to the North Sea) in northern Scotland. Hundreds of people have reported seeing the animal, which is nicknamed Nessie. According to the most common descriptions, the creature has flippers; one or two humps; a thick tapering tail; and a long, slender neck. Some observers believe the Loch Ness Monster may be a long-lost relative of the dinosaurs. Others believe it is more like a manatee or seal. But no scientific evidence has been found to support any of these claims, and most biologists believe Nessie does not exist.

Several scientific expeditions have explored the waters of Loch Ness; yet none of them have produced clear evidence of Nessie's existence. In 2003, an exploration team funded by the British Broadcasting Corporation conducted an extensive search of Loch Ness using sophisticated sonar equipment to detect any underwater objects. The search found no trace of any sea animal resembling the monster. Despite such findings, however, the mystery of the Loch Ness Monster continues to attract many tourists to Loch Ness.

Under the Boardwalk

WORDS BY ARTHUR RESNICK AND KENNY YOUNG

When the sun beats down and burns the tar up on the roof,
And your shoes get so hot you wish your tired feet were fireproof,
Under the boardwalk, down by the sea,
On a blanket with my baby, that's where I'll be.

From the park you hear the happy sound of the carousel,
You can almost taste the hot dogs and french fries they sell,
Under the boardwalk, down by the sea,
On a blanket with my baby, that's where I'll be.

Under the boardwalk, out of the sun
Under the boardwalk, we'll be having some fun
Under the boardwalk, people walking above
Under the boardwalk, we'll be falling in love
Under the boardwalk, boardwalk!

When the Ship Comes In

(An excerpt)

BY BOB DYLAN

Oh the time will come up when the winds will stop
And the breeze will cease to be breathin'.
Like the stillness in the wind 'fore the hurricane begins,
The hour that the ship comes in.

Oh the seas will split and the ship will hit
And the sands on the shoreline will be shaking.
Then the tide will sound and the waves will pound
And the morning will be breaking.

Oh the fishes will laugh as they swim out of the path
And the seagulls they'll be smiling.
And the rocks on the sand will proudly stand,
The hour that the ship comes in.

And the words that are used for to get the ship confused
Will not be understood as they're spoken.
For the chains of the sea will have busted in the night
And will be buried at the bottom of the ocean.

20,000 Leagues Under the Sea

(Excerpts from the Underwater Forest chapter)

BY JULES VERNE

In 20,000 Leagues Under the Sea, *Professor Arronax (who narrates) and his friends Conseil and Ned Land are thrown overboard, and saved/captured by Captain Nemo, the captain and inventor of an amazing submarine called the* Nautilus. *He leads them on many adventures. Here, Captain Nemo guides them through a lush underwater forest.*

We had finally arrived at the edge of this forest, undoubtedly one of the most beautiful in all of Captain Nemo's vast domain. . . .

This forest was composed of large, treelike plants, and as soon as we had gone under its vast arches, I was struck by the strange shape of their branches—a shape I had never seen before.

None of the grass covering the ground nor any of the branches attached to the trees was inclined, bent, or in any way horizontal. Everything rose toward the surface. . . .

I soon became accustomed to this peculiar arrangement of things, as well as to the relative darkness which surrounded us. . . .

I noticed that all the specimens of the vegetable kingdom were only lightly held to the ground. Without roots and not caring whether they are fixed to something solid, sand, shells, or pebbles, they only ask of the ground for something to hang on to, not for their life's blood. These plants are self-propagating, and derive their existence from the water, which sustains and nourishes them. Most of them had, instead of leaves, whimsically shaped blades in a narrow range of colors, comprising only pink, carmine, green, olive, tan, and brown. . . .

Fish flies flew from branch to branch like a flock of hummingbirds, while yellow lepiscanthae with bristling jaws and pointed scales rose at our feet like a flock of snipe.

Toward one in the afternoon, Captain Nemo gave the signal to halt. I was rather pleased to stop, and we stretched out under a bower of alariae with their long ribbons shooting out as straight as arrows.

This short rest delighted me. Nothing was lacking but the charm of conversation. But it was impossible to talk. I brought my large copper helmet near Conseil's. I saw his eyes shining with joy, and to show his satisfaction, he bobbed his head around inside his helmet in the most comical way imaginable.

I was very surprised not to feel very hungry after walking for four hours. . . . But on the other hand, as happens with all divers, I felt an uncontrollable desire to sleep. Soon my eyes closed behind their thick glass windows and I fell into a deep slumber, which till then I had been able to fight off merely by walking. I was thus merely following the example of Captain Nemo and his powerful companion, who had already stretched out and gone to sleep.

There was no way of knowing how long I dozed, but when I awoke it seemed as if the sun were sinking toward the horizon. Captain Nemo had already gotten up, and I was beginning to stretch my limbs when an unexpected sight brought me quickly to my feet.

Only a few steps away, a monstrous spider crab, three feet high, was eying me ready to jump. Although my diving suit was thick enough to protect me from his bite, I could not help shuddering with horror. Just then Conseil and the sailor from the *Nautilus* awoke. Captain Nemo pointed out the hideous crab to his companion, who knocked it away with one blow of his rifle butt. . . .

I supposed that this halt had marked the end of our walk; but I was wrong, and instead of returning to the *Nautilus*, Captain Nemo continued his daring excursion.

The ground continued falling off, but at an even greater angle, taking us deeper and deeper. It must have been around three o'clock when we reached a depth of about five hundred feet in a narrow valley between high, vertical walls. Thanks to the perfection of our diving equipment, we were thus going three hundred feet deeper than men had ever gone before.

I say five hundred feet, even though no instrument permitted me to calculate this depth. But I knew that even in the clearest water the sun's rays penetrate no deeper. And just then the darkness had become almost complete. Ten steps away I could see nothing. I was therefore walking, groping my way alone, when suddenly I saw a bright white light shining ahead. Captain Nemo had just turned on his electric lamp. His companion did the same. Conseil and I followed their example. By turning a screw, I connected the coil to the glass spiral; and the sea, lit by our four lanterns, was illuminated within a radius of eighty feet. . . .

Finally at about four o'clock, this marvelous excursion came to an end. A huge, magnificent wall of rock rose before us, a heap of gigantic blocks, an enormous, unclimbable granite cliff hollowed out with dark caves. . . .

We began the return trip. Captain Nemo had again taken the lead, and continued walking forward without hesitation. It seemed to me that we were not returning to the *Nautilus* by the same path. This new route, very steep and difficult, brought us quickly up toward

the surface. Nevertheless this return to the upper layers of the ocean was not so sudden as to bring about too quick a decompression, which would have done our lungs serious injury. . . . Very soon the light reappeared and grew stronger, and since the sun was already low on the horizon, the refraction again edged every object with a rainbowlike border.

At a depth of thirty feet we walked amid a swarm of little fish of all kinds, more numerous than birds in the air and also more agile. . . .

I also noticed another strange effect. Thick clouds passed by, forming and disappearing rapidly; but when I thought it over, I realized that these so-called clouds were merely due to the varying height of the water in the midst of a ground swell, and when I looked carefully I could see the foam breaking on its crests and spreading over the surface. I could even see the shadows of large birds overhead as they came down and skimmed the water. . . .

For two hours we crossed sandy plains alternating with prairies of seaweed in which it was very difficult to walk. I was at the end of my strength when we finally saw a vague glimmer piercing the darkness of the water a half mile away. It was the *Nautilus*'s light. . . .

A half an hour later, guided by the electric light, we reached the *Nautilus*. . . .

There our diving suits were taken off, although not without some difficulty; and I, exhausted and dying of hunger, went to my room in a state of wonder at our extraordinary excursion in the ocean depths.

Pirate Story

BY ROBERT LOUIS STEVENSON

Three of us afloat in the meadow by the swing,
Three of us aboard in the basket on the lea.
Winds are in the air, they are blowing in the spring,
And waves are on the meadow like the waves there are at sea.

Where shall we adventure, today that we're afloat,
Wary of the weather and steering by a star?
Shall it be to Africa, a-steering of the boat,
To Providence, or Babylon, or off to Malabar?

Hi! but here's a squadron a-rowing on the sea—
Cattle on the meadow a-charging with a roar!
Quick, and we'll escape them, they're mad as they can be,
The wicket is the harbor and the garden is the shore.

The Old Man and the Sea

(An excerpt)

BY ERNEST HEMINGWAY

One of Hemingway's most famous works, The Old Man and the Sea *is about a fisherman who catches an enormous marlin, so big that he must work desperately for days to bring it in. It is as much a struggle with himself as with the fish.*

The sun was rising for the third time since he had put to sea when the fish started to circle.

He could not see by the slant of the line that the fish was circling. It was too early for that. He just felt a faint slackening of the pressure of the line and he commenced to pull on it gently with his right hand. It tightened, as always, but just when he reached the point where it would break, line began to come in. He slipped his shoulders and head from under the line and began to pull in line steadily and gently. He used both of his hands in a swinging motion and tried to do the pulling as much as he could with his body and his legs. His old legs and shoulders pivoted with the swinging of the pulling.

"It is a very big circle," he said. "But he is circling."

Then the line would not come in any more and he held it until he saw the drops jumping from it in the sun. Then it started out and the old man knelt down and let it go grudgingly back into the dark water.

"He is making the far part of his circle now," he said. I must hold all I can, he thought. The strain will shorten his circle each time. Perhaps in an hour I will see him. . . .

But the fish kept on circling slowly and the old man was wet with sweat and tired deep into his bones two hours later. But the circles were much shorter now and from the way the line slanted he could tell the fish had risen steadily while he swam.

For an hour the old man had been seeing black spots. . . . They were normal at the tension that he was pulling on the line. Twice, though, he felt faint and dizzy and that had worried him. . . .

"Don't jump, fish," he said. "Don't jump." . . .

The old man was gaining line steadily now. But he felt faint again. He lifted some seawater with his left hand and put it on his head. Then he put more on and rubbed the back of his neck.

"I have no cramps," he said. "He'll be up soon and I can last. You have to last. Don't even speak of it."

He kneeled against the bow and, for a moment, slipped the line over his back again. I'll rest now while he goes out on the circle and then stand up and work on him when he comes in, he decided.

It was a great temptation to rest in the bow and let the fish make one circle by himself without recovering any line. But when the strain showed the fish had turned to come toward the boat, the old man rose to his feet and started the pivoting and the weaving pulling that brought in all the line he gained. . . .

It was on the third turn that he saw the fish first.

He saw him first as a dark shadow that took so long to pass under the boat that he could not believe its length.

"No," he said. "He can't be that big."

But he was that big and at the end of this circle he came to the surface only thirty yards away and the old man saw his tail out of the water. It was higher than a big scythe blade and very pale lavender above the dark blue water. It raked back and as the fish swam just below the surface the old man could see his huge bulk and the purple stripes that banded him. His dorsal fin was down and his huge pectorals were spread wide. . . .

The old man was sweating now but from something else besides the sun. On each calm placid turn the fish made he was gaining line and he was sure that in two turns more he would have a chance to get the harpoon in.

But I must get him close, close, close, he thought. I mustn't try for the head. I must get the heart.

"Be calm and strong, old man," he said.

On the next circle the fish's back was out but he was too far from the boat. On the next circle he was still too far away but he was higher out of water and the old man was sure that by gaining some more line he could have him alongside.

He had rigged his harpoon long before and its coil of light rope was in a round basket and the end was made fast to the bitt in the bow.

The fish was coming in on his circle now calm and beautiful looking and only his great tail moving. The old man pulled on him all that he could to bring him closer. For just a moment the fish turned a little on his side. Then he straightened himself and began another circle.

"I moved him," the old man said. "I moved him then." . . .

But when he put all of his effort on, starting it well out before the fish came alongside and pulling with all his strength, the fish pulled part way over and then righted himself and swam away. . . .

On the next turn, he nearly had him. But again the fish righted himself and swam slowly away.

You are killing me, fish, the old man thought. But you have a right to. Never have I seen a greater, or more beautiful, or calmer or more noble thing than you, brother. Come on and kill me. I do not care who kills who.

Now you are getting confused in the head, he thought. You must keep your head clear and know how to suffer like a man. Or a fish, he thought.

"Clear up, head," he said in a voice he could hardly hear. "Clear up." . . .

I'll try it again, the old man promised, although his hands were mushy now and he could only see well in flashes. . . .

He took all his pain and what was left of his strength and his long-gone pride and he put it against the fish's agony and the fish came over onto his side and swam gently on his side, his bill almost touching the planking of the skiff and started to pass the boat, long, deep, wide, silver, and barred with purple and interminable in the water.

The old man dropped the line and put his foot on it and lifted the harpoon as high as he could and drove it down with all his strength, and more strength he had just summoned, into the fish's side just behind the great chest fin that rose high in the air to the altitude of the old man's chest. He felt the iron go in and he leaned on it and drove it further and then pushed all his weight after it.

Then the fish came alive, with his death in him, and rose high out of the water showing all his great length and width and all his power and his beauty. He seemed to hang in the air above the old man in the skiff. Then he fell into the water with a crash that sent spray over the old man and over all of the skiff.

The old man felt faint and sick and he could not see well. But he cleared the harpoon line and let it run slowly through his raw hands and, when he could see, he saw the fish was on his back with his silver belly up. . . .

The old man looked carefully in the glimpse of vision that he had. Then he took two turns of the harpoon line around the bitt in the bow and laid his head on his hands.

"Keep my head clear," he said against the wood of the bow. "I am a tired old man. But I have killed this fish which is my brother and now I must do the slave work."

Now I must prepare the nooses and the rope to lash him alongside, he thought. . . . I must prepare everything, then bring him in and lash him well and step the mast and set sail for home.

By the Beautiful Sea

(An excerpt)

WORDS BY HAROLD R. ATTERIDGE

By the sea, by the sea,
By the beautiful sea,
You and I, you and I,
Oh! how happy we'll be.

When each wave comes a-rolling in,
We will duck or swim.
And we'll float and fool
Around the water.

Over and under
And then up for air.
Pa is rich, Ma is rich,
So now what do we care?

I love to be beside your side,
Beside the sea,
Beside the seaside,
By the beautiful sea.

Three Men in a Tub

BY MOTHER GOOSE

Rub a dub dub,
Three men in a tub;
And who do you think they be?
The Butcher, the Baker,
The Candlestick Maker;
Turn 'em out, knaves all three!

Sailing, Sailing

TRADITIONAL LULLABY

Sailing, sailing,
Over the oceans blue.
My Duck brings gifts,
By way of BimBamBoo.

The Rime of the Ancient Mariner

(An excerpt)

BY SAMUEL TAYLOR COLERIDGE

According to nautical lore, an albatross is a sign of good luck for a ship. The mariner in this poem kills an albatross that appears through the fog, and soon after the ship is becalmed. The sailors hang the dead bird around the mariner's neck, hoping to show that it was he alone who did wrong, but the slaying of the albatross brings a horrible curse on everyone on board the ship.

Then all averred, I had killed the bird
That brought the fog and mist.
"'Twas right," said they, "such birds to slay,
That bring the fog and mist."

The fair breeze blew, the white foam flew,
The furrow followed free.
We were the first that ever burst
Into that silent sea.

Down dropt the breeze, the sails
dropt down,
'Twas sad as sad could be.
And we did speak only to break
The silence of the sea!

All in a hot and copper sky,
The bloody sun, at noon,
Right up above the mast did stand,
No bigger than the moon.

Day after day, day after day,
We stuck, nor breath nor motion,
As idle as a painted ship
Upon a painted ocean.

Where Go the Boats?

BY ROBERT LOUIS STEVENSON

Green leaves a-floating,
Castles of the foam,
Boats of mine a-boating—
Where will all come home?

Away down the river,
A hundred miles or more,
Other little children
Shall bring my boats to shore.

Blow the Man Down

POPULAR SEA CHANTEY

Sailing was once a very rough profession, and those sailors who didn't do as they were told were "blown," or knocked, down by their superiors—sometimes with a fist, other times with something heavier. This was particularly common on the Black Ball shipping fleet.

Come all you young fellows that follow
the sea,
With a way, hey, blow the man down,
Now please pay attention and listen to me,
Give me some time to blow the man down.

There are tinkers and tailors, shoemakers
and all,
With a way, hey, blow the man down,
They've all shipped for sailors on board
the Black Ball,
Give me some time to blow the man down.

Puff the Magic Dragon

BY PETER YARROW AND LEONARD LIPTON

Puff, the magic dragon, lived by the sea
And frolicked in the autumn mist in a land called Honah Lee,
Little Jackie Paper loved that rascal Puff
And brought him strings and sealing wax and other fancy stuff.

Together they would travel on a boat with billowed sail
Jackie kept a lookout perched on Puff's gigantic tail,
Noble kings and princes would bow whene'er they came,
Pirate ships would lower their flags when Puff roared out his name.

A dragon lives forever but no so little boys
Painted wings and giant rings make way for other toys.
One gray night it happened, Jackie Paper came no more
And Puff that mighty dragon, he ceased his fearless roar.

His head was bent in sorrow, green scales fell like rain,
Puff no longer went to play along the cherry lane.
Without his lifelong friend, Puff could not be brave,
So Puff that mighty dragon sadly slipped into his cave.

Pebbles

BY E. F. N. (8 YEARS OLD IN 1902)

O little pebbles down by the sea!
I wonder if you are waiting for me?
Shining and dancing in the warm light,
Washed by the waves, and looking
so bright.

Dear little pebbles, white as fresh snow,
I'll tell you something perhaps you
don't know:
The summer is coming, and so are we,
For Papa says we will go to the sea.

Then, pretty pebbles, our little bare feet
Will kiss you again and again, you're
so sweet:
I know you won't scratch us, you're smooth
and round,
Without any "stickers," like those on
the ground.

And I'll tell you another thing, pebbles
so kind:
I will bring—unless Nursey should leave
them behind—
A pail and a shovel; and what will I do?
Is to dig a big hole for a well—
wouldn't you?

And then when the waves come
scampering up,
It will be filled to the top like my own
silver cup:
And we will run down and splash it about,
Till another big wave, with a laugh and
a shout.

Chases us up till we're out of reach—
All of us safe, high and dry on the beach.
Yes, the waves are great fun, but I really
must say
I'd rather have pebbles when I want to play.

O summer, do hurry! O spring, go away!
Little flowers, please blossom! Dear birds,
sing your lay!
And the sooner you do it, the better for me,
For the pebbles are waiting, I know,
by the sea.

SAIDA

Leif Eriksson, Son of Erik the Red

Christopher Columbus is often thought of as the first European explorer to discover the Americas, but in fact, he wasn't. Long before Columbus came to North America in 1492, Vikings had discovered this new land. Leading them was Leif Eriksson, son of Erik the Red.

More than a thousand years ago, the Vikings ruled Norway and Iceland. Stories passed down for hundreds of years describe these men as fierce and war-like pirates who destroyed towns and terrorized people, armed with spears, axes, hooks, ball-and-chains, crossbows, barbed shields, and catapults for launching jagged stones.

Today, scientists have found and studied many places with Viking ruins. Recent discoveries have proven that however fierce the Vikings were, they were also daring and creative. They carved beautiful wooden ships, and in those ships they sailed farther than any other explorers of that time, visiting and trading with many countries.

Erik Thorvaldsson was known as Erik the Red for his bright red hair and long red beard. Erik had a temper as vivid as his hair, and about the year 985 he killed two men in a fight. As punishment, he was banished from his home in Iceland. He sailed away and was not seen for years.

By 990, Erik the Red had been away from his family for a long time. They were certain that he would never return. But Erik the Red did return to Iceland. He came back with tales of a new land across the sea—a new land with green fields, that Erik called Greenland. At the time, Iceland was becoming crowded. So several hundred Vikings agreed to go with Erik to Greenland.

Erik's son Leif grew up in the colony on Greenland, and became quite a good sailor. About the year 997, Erik the Red decided to send Leif to Norway. Leif's ship, loaded with gifts for King Olaf, arrived safely in Norway. King Olaf was pleased with the gifts.

The following year, Leif Eriksson and his crew began the voyage back to Greenland. It was a hard trip with many storms. When the skies cleared, Leif did not recognize the land before him. He realized that his ship had blown far west of Greenland. He turned back east, but he promised himself he would return and explore the new land some day. Some time later, and with about 35 other men, Leif sailed off into the unknown.

After sailing for many weeks with a strong wind, Leif sighted land. He anchored his ship and went on shore. The ground was covered with many trees, green grass and flowers. Grape vines were growing in the meadows.

Leif called this land Vinland, meaning "Land of Vines." Most people believe that Leif Eriksson reached Vinland about the year 1000, about 500 years before Christopher Columbus landed in the New World. Of course, people do not agree on exactly where Leif landed. Some think Leif Eriksson came to shore on the island of Newfoundland, where Viking ruins have been found. Still others think he sailed as far south as New England. Some historians believe that Leif landed near Cape Cod, Massachusetts. But by the time Leif returned to Greenland, Erik the Red had died. Leif was now the ruler of Greenland.

He would never return to Vinland.

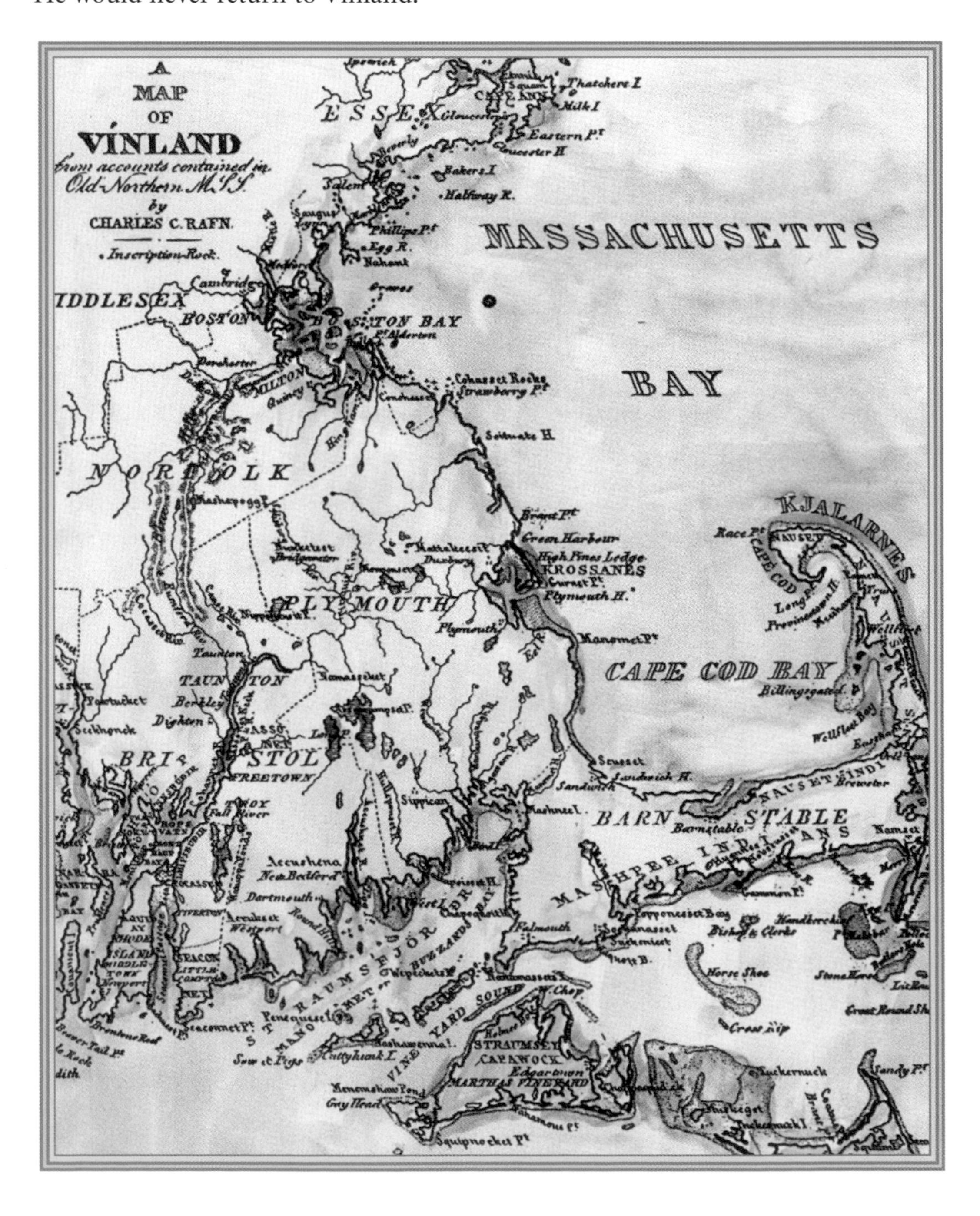

Octopus's Garden

BY RICHARD STARKEY

I'd like to be under the sea
In an Octopus's Garden in the shade.
He'd let us in, knows where we've been
In his Octopus's Garden in the shade.
I'd ask my friends to come and see
An Octopus's Garden with me.
I'd like to be under the sea
In an Octopus's Garden in the shade.

We would be warm below the storm
In our little hideaway beneath the waves.
Resting our head on the sea bed
In an Octopus's Garden near a cave.
We would sing and dance around
Because we know we can't be found.
I'd like to be under the sea
In an Octopus's Garden in the shade.

We would shout and swim about
The coral that lies beneath the waves.
Oh, what joy for every girl and boy
Knowing they're happy and they're safe.
We would be so happy, you and me.
No one there to tell us what to do.
I'd like to be under the sea
In an Octopus's Garden with you.

Jason and the Argonauts

The Greek myths have been told and retold over thousands of years. Many encompass journeys, and the tale of the Argonauts is a long and fascinating one. This is just the beginning:

Prince Jason lost no time in sending messengers to all the cities of Greece to announce that he was going in quest of the Golden Fleece. He would need the help of 49 of the bravest and strongest heroes alive, to row his vessel and face the dangers of the journey. Jason himself would be the fiftieth.

At this news, adventurous youths all over the country set out for Iolchos, hopeful that they could join the quest. Some of them had already fought with giants, and slain dragons. There was a fair prospect that they would meet with more of such adventures before finding the Golden Fleece. Shaking hands with Jason, they assured him that they did not care a pin for their lives, but would help row the vessel to the remotest edge of the world, and as much farther as he might think it best to go.

Many of these brave fellows had been educated by Chiron, the centaur, and were therefore old schoolmates of Jason. The mighty Hercules, who would later hold up the sky, was one of them. And there were Caster and Pollux, the twin brothers; and Theseus, renowned for killing the Minotaur; and Lynceus, with his wonderfully sharp eyes, which could see through a millstone, or look right down through the depths of the earth; and Orpheus, who sang and played upon his lyre so powerfully that he could charm any beast. He could even make the rocks bestir their moss-grown bulk out of the ground, and the forest trees uproot themselves.

Also among the group of heroes was a young Atalanta, who had been nursed among the mountains by a bear. So light of foot was she that she could step from one foamy crest of a wave to the foamy crest of another, without wetting more than the sole of her sandal. And joining her were the two sons of the North Wind, who had wings on their shoulders, and, if the ship were becalmed, could puff out their cheeks, and blow almost as strong a breeze as their father.

Jason appointed Tiphys to be helmsman, because he was a stargazer, and knew the points of the compass. Lynceus, on account of his sharp sight, was stationed as a lookout in the prow, where he saw a whole day's sail ahead. Lynceus could tell exactly what kind of rocks or sands were at the bottom of the sea they sailed over; and he often cried out to his companions that they were sailing over heaps of sunken treasure, sunk so deeply that it could not be recovered.

These fifty brave adventurers were called the Argonauts, sailors on the *Argo*, but when the heroes attempted to set off, the ship herself refused to move. They pushed and strained, but the *Argo* would not slip into the sea. At last, quite wearied out, they sat themselves down on the shore.

Jason called out to the galley's figurehead, a woman carved from a branch of the magic oak of Dodona.

"O daughter of the Talking Oak," cried he, "how shall we set to work to get our vessel into the water?"

"Seat yourselves," answered the image, "seat yourselves, and handle your oars, and let Orpheus play upon his harp."

Immediately the fifty heroes got on board, and seizing their oars, held them in the air, while Orpheus swept his fingers across the lyre. At the first ringing note they felt the vessel stir, and the galley slid at once into the sea, dipping her prow and rising again as buoyant as a swan. The rowers plied their fifty oars; the white foam boiled up before the prow; the water gurgled and bubbled in their wake; the vessel seemed to dance over the billows. Thus, triumphantly, did the *Argo* sail out of the harbor to begin the adventures of the Argonauts.

The Water-Babies

(An excerpt)

BY CHARLES KINGSLEY

In The Water-Babies, *Tom is a young chimney sweep who is magically changed into a water creature. He meets many creatures in this vivid fantasy—here, he encounters two noble salmon.*

Such a fish! Shining silver from his head to tail and here and there a crimson dot; with a grand hooked nose and grand curling lip, and a grand bright eye, looking 'round him as proudly as a king, and surveying the water right and left as if all belonged to him. Surely he must be the salmon, the king of all the fish.

Tom was so frightened that he longed to creep into a hole, but he need not have been; for salmon are all true gentlemen, and, like true gentlemen, they look noble and proud enough, and yet, like true gentlemen, they never harm or quarrel with anyone, but go about their own business, and leave rude fellows to themselves.

The salmon looked at him full in the face, and then went on without minding him, with a swish or two of his tail, which made the stream boil again. And in a few minutes came another, and then four or five, and so on; and all passed Tom, rushing and plunging up the cataract with strong strokes of their silver tails, now and then leaping clean out of water and up over a rock, shining gloriously for a moment in the bright sun; while Tom was so delighted that he could have watched them all day long.

And at last one came up bigger than all the rest, but he came slowly, and stopped, and looked back, and seemed very anxious and busy. And Tom saw that he was helping another salmon, an especially handsome one, who had not a single spot upon it, but was clothed in pure silver from nose to tail.

"My dear," said the great fish to his companion, "you really look dreadfully tired, and you must not overexert yourself at first. Do rest yourself behind this rock," and he shoved her gently with his nose, to the rock where Tom sat.

You must know that this was the salmon's wife. For salmon, like other true gentlemen, always choose their lady, and love her, and are true to her, and take care of her and work for her, and fight for her, as every true gentlemen ought; and are not like vulgar chub and roach and pike, who have no high feelings, and take no care of their wives.

Then he saw Tom, and looked at him very fiercely one moment, as if he was going to bite him.

"What do you want here?" he said, very fiercely.

"Oh, don't hurt me!" cried Tom. "I only want to look at you; you are so handsome."

"Ah!" said the salmon, very stately but very civilly. "I really beg your pardon; I see what you are, my little dear. I have met one or two creatures like you before, and found them very agreeable and well behaved. Indeed, one of them showed me a great kindness lately, which I hope to be able to repay. I hope we shall not be in your way here. As soon as this lady is rested, we shall proceed on our journey."

What a well-bred old salmon he was!

"So you have seen things like me before?" asked Tom.

"Several times, my dear. Indeed, it was only last night that one at the river's mouth came and warned me and my wife of some new stake nets which had got into the stream, I cannot tell how, since last winter, and showed us the way 'round them, in the most charming obliging way."

"So there are babies in the sea?" cried Tom, and clapped his little hands. "Then I shall have someone to play with there? How delightful!"

"Were there no babies up this stream?" asked the lady salmon.

"No! and I grew so lonely. I thought I saw three last night, but they were gone in an instant, down to the sea. So I went too, for I had nothing to play with but caddises and dragonflies and trout."

"Ugh!" cried the lady, "what low company!"

"My dear, if he has been in low company, he has certainly not learnt their low manners," said the salmon.

"No, indeed, poor little dear; But how sad for him to live among such people as caddises, who have actually six legs, the nasty things, and dragonflies, too! Why, they are not even good to eat, for I tried them once, and they are hard and empty; and, as for trout, everyone knows what they are." Where whereon she curled up her lip, and looked dreadfully scornful, while her husband curled up his too, till he looked as proud as Alcibiades.

"Why do you dislike the trout so?" asked Tom.

"My dear, we do not even mention them, if we can help it; for I am sorry to say they are relations of ours who do us no credit. A great many years ago they were just like us, but they were so lazy, and cowardly, and greedy, that instead of going down to the sea every year to see the world and grow strong and fat, they chose to stay and poke about in the little streams and eat worms and grubs; and they are very properly punished for it, for they have grown ugly and brown and spotted and small, and are actually so degraded in their tastes, that they will eat our children."

"And then they pretend to scrape acquaintance with us again," said the lady. "Why, I have actually known one of them to propose to a lady salmon, the impudent little creature."

"I should hope," said the gentleman, "that there are very few ladies who would degrade themselves by listening to such a creature for an instant. If I saw such a thing happen, I should consider it my duty to put them both to death upon the spot." So the old salmon said, like an old blue-blooded hidalgo of Spain; and what is more, he would have done it, too. For you must know, no enemies are so bitter against each other as those who are of the same race; and a salmon looks on a trout as some great folks look on some little folks, as something just too much like himself to be tolerated.

About Two Little Boys

BY K. A. M.

Two little boys, all neat and clean,
Came down upon the shore;
They did not know old Ocean's ways—
They'd ne'er seen him before.

So quietly they sat them down,
To build a fort of sand;
Their backs were turned upon the sea,
Their faces toward the land.

They had just built a famous fort—
The handkerchief was spread—
When up there came a stealthy wave,
And turned them heels over head.

I Saw Three Ships

TRADITIONAL ENGLISH CAROL

I saw three ships a-sailing by,
On Christmas Day, on Christmas Day.
I saw three ships a-sailing by,
On Christmas Day in the morning.

The Virgin Mary and Christ were there,
On Christmas Day, on Christmas Day.
The Virgin Mary and Christ were there,
On Christmas Day in the morning.

Captain Kidd's Farewell to the Seas

(An excerpt)

TRADITIONAL ENGLISH BALLAD

Captain Kidd is perhaps the most famous pirate in history. According to popular tradition, he and his crew committed every crime possible. He is said to have buried a fabulous pirate treasure that he was never able to go back for, and to have said this as he stood on the gallows:

My name was Captain Kidd, when I sailed, when I sailed,
And so wickedly I did, God's laws I did forbid,
When I sailed, when I sailed.
I roamed from sound to sound, and many a ship I found,
And then I sunk or burned, when I sailed.
I murdered William Moore, and laid him in his gore,
Not many leagues from shore, when I sailed.
Farewell to young and old, all jolly seamen bold,
You're welcome to my gold, for I must die, I must die.
Farewell to London town, the pretty girls all round,
No pardon can be found, and I must die, I must die.

Why the Sea Is Salt

AUTHOR UNKNOWN

Once upon a time in the old, old days there were two brothers, one of whom was rich and the other poor. When Christmas Eve came the poor brother had not a morsel in the house; and so he went to his rich brother and asked for a trifle for Christmas. It was not the first time the brother had helped him, but he was always very close-fisted, and was not particularly glad to see him this time.

"If you'll do what I tell you, you shall have Christmas porridge," he said. The poor brother promised he would, and was very grateful into the bargain.

"Take this bouquet of honeysuckle, and now go to the wizard!" said the rich brother, "and give him the flowers."

"Well, what I have promised I must do," said the poor brother. So he took the honeysuckle and set out. He walked and walked the whole day, and as it was getting dark he came to a place where the lights were shining brightly.

"This is most likely the place," thought the man with the flowers.

In a woodshed stood an old man with a long white beard, cutting firewood for Christmas.

"Good evening," said he with the honeysuckle bouquet.

"Good evening to you," said the man. "Where are you going so late?"

"I've come looking for the wizard—that is to say, if I am on the right way," answered the poor man.

"Yes, you are quite right; this is his place," said the old man. "When you get in, the wizard will want to buy your honeysuckle, for flowers are scarce in these parts; but you must not sell them unless you get the hand-quern, which will grind anything you ask it."

The man with the honeysuckle thanked him for all the information, and knocked at the door.

When he got in, it happened just as the old man had said. All the wizard's imps, both big and small, flocked around him like ants, and the wizard offered him one precious thing after another in exchange for the flowers.

"Well," said the man, "my good wife and I were to have these beautiful flowers on our Christmas Eve table, but since you want them so badly I will let you have them. But if I am going to part with the bouquet, I want that hand-quern, which stands behind the door."

The wizard did not like to part with it, and higgled and haggled with the man, but the man stuck to what he had said, and in the end the wizard gave him the quern.

The man set out homeward as quickly as he could; but he did not get home till the clock struck twelve on Christmas Eve.

"Where in all the world have you been?" said his wife. "Here have I been sitting, hour after hour, waiting for you, and have not had as much as two chips to lay on the fire and nothing at all to put into the porridge pot."

"Well, I couldn't get back sooner," said the man. "I have had a good many things to do, and I've had a long way to walk as well; but now I'll show you something," said he, and put the quern on the table.

"Grind herrings and broth, and do it quickly and well," said the man, and magically the quern began to bring forth herrings and broth and filled his own and his wife's dish and then all the rest of the dishes, plates, cups, and then all the pots and tubs, and afterward began flooding the whole kitchen.

The man and his wife were flabbergasted! They fiddled and fumbled and tried to stop the quern, but however much they twisted and turned it, the quern went on grinding, for the man had not asked the woodcutter how to stop it. In a little while the herrings and broth reached so high that the man and his wife were very near drowning. The wife then pulled open the back door, and they rushed out, but herrings and broth came pouring out after them, like a stream, down the dark fields and meadows.

It wasn't long before the stream of broth with herrings tossing about in it filled the entire valley and began to approach the sea. The man and his wife were running in front of it all, and the quern itself was floating upon it all, still grinding away!

Right then a large sailing ship appeared on the shoreline. Its skipper was there silhouetted by the moonlight sampling the herrings and broth. "Not bad, not bad at all," he said, "but it could certainly stand a little salt."

The skipper's crew managed to pluck the quern and the man and his wife out of the herrings and broth, and brought them on board the ship. The skipper turned to the quern and said, "Grind salt, and that both quickly and well," and the quern began to grind out salt so that it spurted to all sides.

When the skipper felt he had enough salt, he wanted to stop the quern, but however much he tried and whatever he did, the quern went on grinding, and the mound of salt grew higher and higher, and at last the ship sank.

And there at the bottom of the sea stands the quern, still grinding salt to this very day, and that is the reason why the sea is salt.

In Fourteen Hundred Ninety-Two

AUTHOR UNKNOWN

In fourteen hundred ninety-two,
Columbus sailed the ocean blue.
He had three ships and left from Spain,
He sailed through sunshine, wind and rain,
Found the New World for me and you.

The Little Mermaid

(An excerpt)

BY HANS CHRISTIAN ANDERSEN

Far out at sea the water is as blue as the petals of the prettiest cornflower and as clear as the purest glass. But it's very deep, deeper than any anchor can reach. . . .

Down in the deepest spot of all is the castle of the sea king. Its walls are built of coral, and the long, pointed windows are made of the clearest amber. . . .

The sea king had been a widower for some years, and his aged mother kept house for him. She was an intelligent woman, but proud when it came to her noble birth. . . . Otherwise,

she deserved great praise, for she was very devoted to her granddaughters, the little sea princesses. They were six pretty children, but the youngest was the loveliest of them all. Her skin was as clear and delicate as a rose leaf. Her eyes were as blue as the deepest sea. . . .

All day long the sea princesses played in the great halls of the castle, where flowers grew right out of the walls. The large amber windows were open, and the fish swam in, just as swallows fly into our homes when we open the windows. The fish glided right up to the princesses, fed from their hands, and waited to be patted.

Outside the castle there was a beautiful garden with trees of deep blue and fiery red. Each of the little princesses had her own plot in the garden, where she could dig and plant as she pleased. . . . While her sisters decorated their gardens with the wonderful things they obtained from sunken ships, the youngest would have nothing but rose-red flowers that were like the sun high above, and a beautiful marble statue. The statue was of a handsome boy, chiseled from pure white stone, and it had come down to the bottom of the sea after a shipwreck.

Nothing pleased the princess more than to hear about the world of humans above the sea. Her old grandmother had to tell her all she knew of the ships and towns, the people and the animals.

"When you are fifteen," the grandmother told the princesses, "we will let you rise to the surface and sit on the rocks in the moonlight while the great ships sail past. You will see both forests and towns."

None of the mermaids was more curious than the youngest, and she, who was so silent and thoughtful, also had the longest wait. Many a night she stood at the open window and gazed up through the dark blue waters, where the fish splash with their fins and tails. She could see the moon and the stars, even though their light was rather pale. . . .

Before the approach of a storm, when they expected a shipwreck, the sisters would swim in front of the vessel and sing sweetly of the delights to be found in the depths of the sea. . . .

W HEATH ROBINSON

When the sisters floated up, arm in arm, through the water in this way, their youngest sister would always stay back all alone, gazing after them. She would have cried, but mermaids have no tears and suffer even more than we do. "Oh, if only I were fifteen years old," she would say. I know that I will love the world up there and all the people who live in it."

Then, at last, she turned fifteen. . . .

She rose through the water as lightly and clearly as a bubble moves to the surface. The sun had just set as she lifted her head above the waves, but the clouds were still tinted with crimson and gold. Up in the pale, pink sky the evening star shone clear and bright. The air was mild and fresh, and the sea dead calm. A large three-masted ship was drifting in the water, with only one sail hoisted because not a breath of wind was stirring. The sailors were lolling about in the rigging and on the yards. There was music and singing on board, and when it grew dark, a hundred lanterns were lit. With their many colors, it looked as if the flags of all nations were fluttering in the air.

The little mermaid swam right up to the porthole of the cabin, and every time a wave lifted her up she could see a crowd of well-dressed people through the clear glass. Among them was a young prince, the handsomest person there, with large dark eyes. He could not have been more that sixteen. It was his birthday, and that's why there was so much of a stir. When the young prince came out on the deck, where the sailors were dancing, more than a hundred rockets swished up into the sky and broke into a glitter, making the sky as bright as day.

The little mermaid was so startled that she dove down under the water. But she quickly popped her head out again. And look! It was just as if all the stars up in heaven were falling down on her. She had never seen fireworks. . . . The ship itself was so brightly illuminated that you could see not only everyone there but even the smallest piece of rope. How handsome the young prince looked as he shook hands with the sailors! He laughed and smiled as the music sounded through the lovely night air.

It grew late, but the little mermaid could not take her eyes off the ship or the handsome prince. The colored lanterns had been extinguished; the rockets no longer rose in the air; and the cannon had ceased firing. But the sea had become restless, and you could hear a moaning, grumbling sound beneath the waves. Still, the mermaid stayed in the water, rocking up and down so that she could look into the cabin. The ship gathered speed; one after another of its sails was unfurled. The waves rose higher, heavy clouds darkened the sky, and lightning flashed in the distance. A dreadful storm was brewing. So the sailors took in the sails, while the great ship rocked and scudded through the raging sea. The waves rose higher and higher until they were like huge black mountains, threatening to bring down the mast.

The little mermaid suddenly realized that the ship was in danger. She herself had to be careful of the beams and bits of wreckage drifting in the water. One moment it was so dark that she could not see a thing, but then a flash of lightning lit up everyone on board. Now it was every man for himself. She was looking for the young prince, and, just as the ship was being torn apart, she saw him disappear into the depths of the sea. . . . No, no, he must not die. So she swam in among the drifting beams and planks, oblivious to the danger of being crushed. She dove deep down and came right back up again among the waves, and at last she found the young prince. He could hardly swim any longer in the stormy sea. His limbs were failing him, his beautiful eyes were closed, and he would certainly have drowned if the little mermaid had not come to his rescue. She held his head above water and then let the waves carry her along with him.

By morning the storm had died down, and there was not a trace of the ship. The sun rose red and glowing up out of the water and seemed to bring color back into the prince's cheeks, but his eyes remained closed. The mermaid kissed his fine, high forehead and smoothed back his wet hair. He seemed to her like the marble statue in her little garden. She kissed him again and made a wish that he might live.

Soon the mermaid saw the mainland before her. . . . The sea formed a small bay at this point, and the water in it was quite still, though very deep. The mermaid swam with the handsome prince to the beach, which was covered with fine, white sand. There she placed him in the warm sunshine, making a pillow for his head with the sand. . . .

Then she watched to see who would come to help the poor prince.

Moses Parts the Red Sea

One of the most dramatic stories of the Old Testament is this one, which demonstrates how powerful God is—so powerful that even the mighty sea cannot stand before him.

Led by Moses, six hundred thousand Israelites walked out of Egypt to Succoth. From Succoth they went south to Etham and north to Baal-Zephon at the edge of the Red Sea. A column of clouds swirled before them by day and a pillar of fire led them by night.

"I have made a terrible mistake," Pharaoh said after the Israelites left. "I must get them back," and he sent six hundred chariots after them.

With an Egyptian army pursuing them from behind, and a great sea lying before them, the desperate Israelites cried out to Moses, "Have you led us this far only to have us die?"

Moses told them that God would rescue them, and he did. "Lift thou up thy rod," he told Moses, "and stretch out thy hand over the sea, and divide it; and the children of Israel shall go into the midst of the sea on dry ground."

A thunderous, windy storm lashed the sea. Moses pointed his wood staff at the water, and it parted. The Israelites raced on dry ground through the walls of water to the safety of the other side. Pharaoh's army chased after them, but when the Egyptian troops were between the walls of water, Moses waved his wood staff and the sea fell in upon them.

Moon Fishing

BY LISEL MUELLER

When the moon was full they came to
the water,
Some with pitchforks, some with rakes,
Some with sieves and ladles
And one with a silver cup.

And they fished till a traveler passed
them and said,
"Fools, to catch the moon you must let
your women
Spread their hair on the water—
Even the wily moon will leap to
that bobbing
Net of shimmering threads,
Grasp and flop till its silver scales
Lie black and still at your feet."

And they fished with the hair of
their women
Till a traveler passed them and said,
"Fools, do you think the moon is caught
lightly,
With glitter and silk threads?
You must cut out your hearts and bait
your hooks
With those dark animals;
What matter you lose your hearts to reel in
your dream?"

And they fished with their tight, hot hearts
Till a traveler passed them and said,
"Fools, what good is the moon to a
heartless man?
Put back your hearts and get on your knees
And drink as you never have,
Until your throats are coated with silver
And your voices ring like bells."

And they fished with their lips and tongues
Until the water was gone
And the moon had slipped away
In the soft, bottomless mud.

20,000 Leagues Under the Sea

(Excerpts from the Giant Squid chapter)

BY JULES VERNE

Giant squid (Architeuthis dux) *can grow to almost 60 feet long and weigh nearly a ton, and it was stories of these animals that inspired Jules Verne to write this passage. Giant squid are, however, uncommon, and generally not interested in attacking submarines.*

Ned Land rushed to the window.

"What a horrible creature!" he cried.

I then looked around, and I could not repress a gesture of repulsion. Before my eyes wriggled a terrible monster worthy of all the legends about such creatures.

It was a giant squid twenty-five feet long. It was heading toward the *Nautilus*, swimming backward very fast. Its huge immobile eyes were of a blue-green color. The eight arms, or rather legs, coming out of its head—it is this which has earned it the name of "cephalopod"—were twice as long as its body and were twisting about like the hair of a Greek fury. We could clearly make out the 250 suckers lining the inside of its tentacles, some of which fastened onto the glass panel of the lounge. This monster's mouth—a horny beak like that of a parakeet—opened and closed vertically. Its tongue, also made of a horn-like substance and armed with several rows of sharp teeth, would come out and shake what seemed like a veritable cutlery. What a whim of nature! A bird's beak in a mollusk! Its elongated body, with a slight swelling in the middle, formed a fleshy mass that must have weighed between forty and fifty thousand pounds. Its color, which could change very fast according to the animal's mood, would vary from a ghastly gray to reddish brown.

What was irritating this creature? Undoubtedly it was the presence of the *Nautilus*, which was more formidable than it and on which its arms and suckers could get no hold. Yet what monsters are such squid! What vitality the Creator has given them, and what vigor of movement! And to think they possess three hearts!

We had encountered this mollusk quite by chance, and I did not want to lose the opportunity of studying it carefully. I overcame my horror at the sight of it, and taking up a pencil, started to draw it.

"This is perhaps the same one they almost caught on the *Alecton*," said Conseil.

"No," replied the Canadian, "because this one's whole, and the other one had lost his tail!"

"That doesn't make any difference," I said. "The arms and tails of these creatures can

re-form by a special process, and I'm sure that in seven years Bouguer's squid has had time to grow another tail."

"Besides," said Ned, "if it isn't this one, it's maybe one of those!"

And in fact, other squid had appeared outside the starboard window. I counted seven. They were swimming in the procession around the *Nautilus* and I could hear the noise of their beaks grinding on the steel hull. Our wishes were more than satisfied.

I continued my work. These monsters kept up with us so easily that they seemed immobile, and I could easily have traced a reduced outline of one on the window. Besides, we were not traveling very fast.

Suddenly the *Nautilus* stopped. There was a blow that made it quiver throughout its length.

"Have we struck ground?" I asked.

"If we did, we're already free," replied the Canadian, "for we're floating."

But even though the *Nautilus* was floating, it wasn't moving. The blades of its propeller were not revolving in the water. After a minute or so, Captain Nemo entered the lounge followed by the first mate.

I had not seen him for some time. He seemed gloomy. Without saying a word to us—perhaps without even seeing us—he went over to the glass panel, looked at the squid and said several words to his first mate, who then left the room. Soon the panels closed and the ceiling lights came on.

I went over to the captain. "A curious collection of squid," I said in the offhand tone of voice of someone standing before the window of an aquarium.

"Indeed it is, Monsieur," he replied, " and we're going to fight them hand to hand."

I looked at the captain. I thought I had not heard him right. "Hand to hand?" I repeated.

"Yes, Monsieur. The propeller has been stopped. I think one of these squids got his horned beak caught up in the propeller, and now we can't move."

"What do you intend to do?"

"Surface the ship and wipe out all this vermin."

"That will be difficult."

"Yes, it will. Our electric bullets have no effect against these animals, for their soft flesh doesn't offer enough resistance to make them explode. But we'll attack them with axes."

"And with a harpoon, Monsieur," said the Canadian, "if you'll permit me to help you."

"I accept, Master Land."

"We'll go with you," I said, and we followed Captain Nemo to the central companionway.

There, ten or twelve men armed with boarding axes were ready for the attack. Conseil and I each took an ax, and Ned Land a harpoon.

By then the *Nautilus* had surfaced. One of the sailors at the top of the companionway unscrewed the bolts holding down the hatch. But hardly had they been unscrewed when the hatch flew up with great violence, obviously pulled up by the suckers on the squid's arm. . . .

With what a fury we then attacked these monsters! We were beyond ourselves. Ten or twelve squid had invaded the platform and sides of the *Nautilus*. . . . But suddenly my brave companion was knocked over by the tentacles of a monster he could not avoid.

Oh, how close my heart came to breaking from emotion and horror! The squid's huge mouth had opened over Ned Land. The poor man was about to be cut in two. I rushed over to help him, but Captain Nemo had gotten there first. He buried his ax between the two enormous jaws, and Ned Land, miraculously saved, got up and plunged his harpoon deep onto the creature's triple heart. . . .

The struggle had lasted fifteen minutes. The monsters, defeated, finally left us and disappeared beneath the surface.

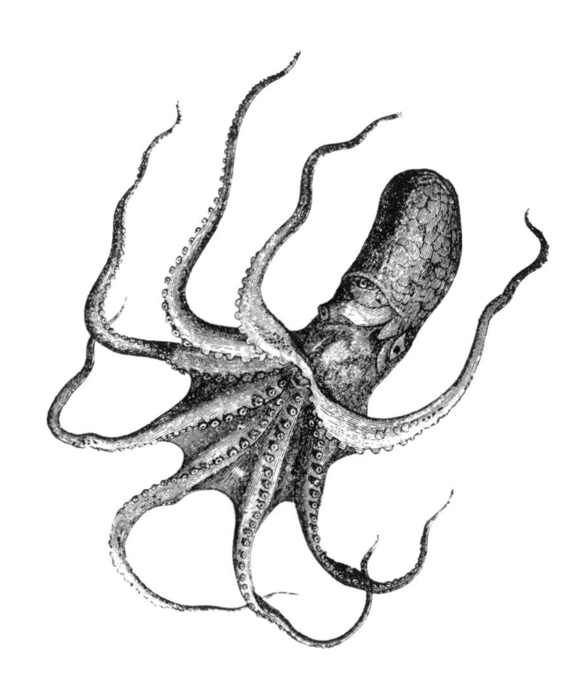

Message in a Bottle

BY WILLIAM STAFFORD

Pull the bow:
A gentle motion.
The stars will do the rest.

Jamaica Farewell

BY ERVING BURGESS

Down the way where the nights are gay
And the sun shines brightly on the
    mountain top
I took a trip on a sailing ship
And when I reached Jamaica I made a stop.

But I'm sad to say that I'm on my way
Won't be back for many a day
My heart is down, my head is
    turning around
Had to leave a little girl in Kingston town.

Sounds of laughter everywhere
And the dancers swinging to and fro
I must declare that my heart is there
Tho' I've been from Maine to Mexico.

But I'm sad to say that I'm on my way
Won't be back for many a day
My heart is down, my head is
    turning around
Had to leave a little girl in Kingston town.

Popeye the Sailor Man

BY SAMMY LERNER

I'm Popeye the Sailor Man,
I'm Popeye the Sailor Man,
I'm strong to the finich, 'cause I eats
me spinach,
I'm Popeye the Sailor Man.

I'm one tough Gazookus which hates
all Palookas,
What ain't on the up and square,
I biffs 'em and buffs 'em and always
outroughs 'em,
But none of them gets nowhere.

If anyone dasses to risk me fisks,
It's boff and it's wham . . . understand?
So keep good behav'our, that's your one
life saver
With Popeye the Sailor Man,
Toot, toot!

Peter Pan

(Excerpts from Captain Hook passages)

BY SIR J. M. BARRIE

Pirates are supposed to be both fearsome and fearless, but in Peter Pan *sometimes they are neither. Smee has a homey, comforting quality, and even villainous Captain Hook, as we see below, sometimes worries in his heart that he ought to be more sportsmanlike, and secretly suspects what we know to be true: that he is, in fact, a coward.*

One green light squinting over Kidd's Creek, which is near the mouth of the pirate river, marked where the brig, the *Jolly Roger*, lay, low in the water; a rakish-looking craft foul to the hull, every beam in her detestable like ground strewn with mangled feathers. She was the cannibal of the seas, and scarce needed that watchful eye, for she floated immune in the horror of her name.

She was wrapped in the blanket of night, through which no sound from her could have reached the shore. There was little sound, and none agreeable save the whir of the ship's sewing machine at which Smee sat, ever industrious and obliging, the essence of the commonplace, pathetic Smee. . . .

Hook trod the deck in thought. O man unfathomable. It was his hour of triumph. Peter had been removed forever from his path, and all the other boys were on the brig, about to walk the plank. It was his grimmest deed since the days when he had brought Barbecue to heel . . . could we be surprised had he now paced the deck unsteadily, bellied out by the winds of his success?

But there was no elation in his gait, which kept pace with the action of his somber mind. Hook was profoundly dejected.

He was often thus when communing with himself on board ship in the quietude of the night. It was because he was so terribly alone. This inscrutable man never felt more alone than when surrounded by his dogs. They were socially so inferior to him.

Hook was not his true name. To reveal who he really was would even at this date set the country in a blaze; but as those who read between the lines must already have guessed, he had been at a famous public school; and its traditions still clung to him . . . and he still adhered in his walk to the school's distinguished slouch. But above all he retained the passion for good form.

Good form! However much he may have degenerated, he still knew that this is all that really matters. . . .

Most disquieting reflection of all, was it not bad form to think about good form?

His vitals were tortured by this problem. It was a claw within him sharper than the iron one; and as it tore him, the perspiration dripped down his sallow countenance and streaked his doublet. Ofttimes he drew his sleeve across his face, but there was no damming that trickle.

Ah, envy not Hook.

There came to him a presentiment of his early dissolution. . . . Hook felt a gloomy desire to make his dying speech, lest presently there should be no time for it.

"Better for Hook," he cried, "if he had had less ambition." It was in his darkest hours only that he referred to himself in the third person.

"No little children to love me."

Strange that he should think of this, which had never troubled him before; perhaps the sewing machine brought it to his mind. For long he muttered to himself, staring at Smee, who was hemming placidly, under the conviction that all children feared him.

Feared him! Feared Smee! There was not a child on board the brig that night who did not already love him. He had said horrid things to them and hit them with the palm of his hand because he could not hit with his fist; but they had only clung to him the more. Michael had tried on his spectacles.

To tell poor Smee that they thought him lovable! Hook itched to do it, but it seemed too brutal. Instead, he revolved this mystery in his mind: why do they find Smee lovable? He pursued the problem like the sleuth-hound that he was. If Smee was lovable, what was it that made him so? A terrible answer suddenly presented itself: "Good form?"

Had the bo'sun good form without knowing it, which is the best form of all? . . .

With a cry of rage he raised his iron hand over Smee's head; but he did not tear. What arrested him was this reflection:

"To claw a man because he is good form, what would that be?"

"Bad form!"

The Boat

BY ROBERT PACK

I dressed my father in his little clothes,
Blue sailor suit, brass buttons on his coat.
He asked me where the running
water goes.

"Down to the sea," I said; "Set it afloat!"
Beside the stream he bent and raised
the sail,
Uncurled the string and launched the
painted boat.

White birds, flown like flags, wrenched
his eyes pale.
He leaped on the tight deck and took
the wind.
I watched the ship foam lurching in
the gale,
And cried, "Come back, you don't know
what you'll find!"
He steered. The ship grew, reddening
the sky.
Water throbbed backward, blind
stumbling after blind.

The rusty storm diminished in his eye,
And down he looked at me. A harbor rose.
I asked, "What happens, Father, when
you die?"

He told where all the running water goes,
And dressed me gently in my little clothes.

Poseidon, God of the Sea

People have always been awed by the power and magic of the sea, so it's not surprising that one of the Greek's most powerful gods was Poseidon.

Zeus, Poseidon, and Hades divided up the world among them. Zeus ruled the sky, Hades the dark underworld, and Poseidon had lordship over the sea. Known as Neptune to the Romans, he was a god of enormous strength. With his three-pronged trident, he could strike the earth and make earthquakes. Poseidon is said to have created the first horses by striking a rock with his trident, and horses were considered sacred to him. Also among his creations were Pegasus, the winged horse, and many frightening sea monsters. He is said to live in a golden palace at the bottom of the sea.

In Praise of Sailing

BY WELLERAN POLTARNEES

The rightness and beauty of a boat, venturing forth on great waters with only the winds and tides to carry it, is one of life's supreme pleasures. Our delight in this comes from deep within. The rivers, the lakes, the seas call us with their mysteries.

To sail is to escape to a place apart from our daily world. It invites adventure. We have learned that the sea is a living being, and that the mastery of a boat involves cooperation, and the skillful application of our inheritance of sailing lore.

The vessels are wonderful to behold whether they be slight or majestic, old or new. It is a marvel how the sails are crafted to take and hold the wind, and the hulls to cleave the waters. Gentle days on the water fill us with peace, and heavy seas test our abilities and our courage.

Days on the water offer enchantments to the body, the mind, the spirit, and we who sail enjoy, in our boats, the sweetest kind of freedom.

Moby-Dick

(Excerpts)

BY HERMAN MELVILLE

Melville wrote Moby-Dick *in stylized prose that approaches poetry. It is considered one of the great classics of English literature. Captain Ahab is the captain of the* Pequod, *a whaling vessel. While hunting whales, Ahab comes across a great, albino sperm whale—Moby Dick. The encounter costs Ahab his leg, and, driven mad by the desire for revenge, he sets out to catch Moby Dick and kill him. Starbuck is the ship's first mate; Tashtego is the ship's harpooner. Here, the crew of the* Pequod *have finally tracked Moby Dick down. Moby Dick has struck the ship and the hull is beginning to take on water. Starbuck begs Captain Ahab to give up, but Ahab, in a separate, smaller boat, will not listen. He calls out to his sinking ship and throws the harpoon at Moby Dick, but even as the whale is hit, the harpoon line catches Ahab, and he is pulled into the sea to his death.*

"Oh! Ahab," cried Starbuck, "not too late is it, even now, the third day, to desist. See! Moby Dick seeks thee not. It is thou, thou, that madly seekest him!" . . .

Diving beneath the settling ship, the whale ran quivering along its keel; but turning under water, swiftly shot to the surface again, far off the other bow, but within a few yards of Ahab's boat, where, for a time, he lay quiescent.

"I turn my body from the sun. What ho, Tashtego! Let me hear thy hammer. Oh! Ye three unsurrendered spires* of mine; thou uncracked keel; and only god-bullied hull; thou firm deck, and haughty helm, and pole-pointed prow, death-glorious ship! Must ye then perish, and without me? Am I cut off from the last fond pride of meanest shipwrecked captains**? Oh, lonely death on lonely life! Oh, now I feel my topmost greatness lies in my topmost grief. Ho, ho! From all your furthest bounds, pour ye now in, ye bold billows of my whole foregone life, and top this one piled comber of my death! Toward thee I roll, thou all-destroying but unconquering whale; to the last I grapple with thee; from hell's heart I stab at thee; for hate's sake I spit my last breath at thee. Sink all coffins and all hearses to one common pool! And since neither can be mine, let me then tow to pieces, while still chasing thee, though tied to thee, thou damned whale! *Thus,* I give up the spear!"

* The three spires are the three masts of the *Pequod*.

** If a captain must die, he hopes to go down with his ship.

The harpoon was darted; the stricken whale flew forward; with igniting velocity the line ran though the groove; ran foul. Ahab stooped to clear it; he did clear it; but the flying turn caught him round the neck, and voicelessly as Turkish mutes bowstring their victim, he was shot out of the boat, ere the crew knew he was gone. Next instant, the heavy eye-splice in the rope's final end flew out of the stark-empty tub, knocked down an oarsman, and smiting the sea, disappeared in the depths.

The Great Sea

BY UVWNUK, ESKIMO

The great sea has set me in motion,
Set me adrift,
Moving me like a weed in a river.

The sky and the strong wind
Have moved my spirit inside me
Till I am carried away
Trembling with joy.

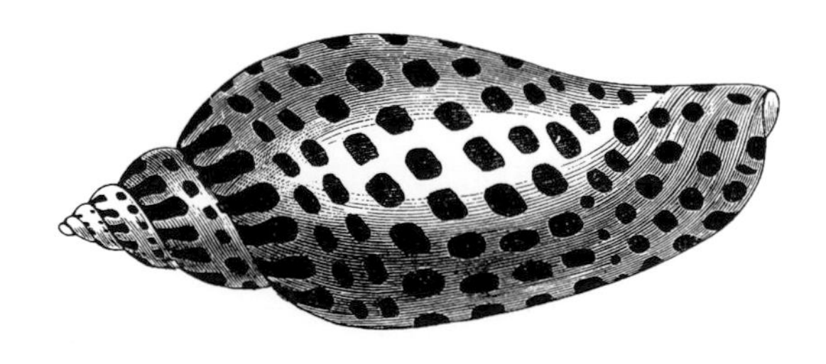

Robinson Crusoe

(Excerpts)

BY DANIEL DEFOE

Robinson Crusoe *is the story of a sailor who is shipwrecked on an island off of South America. He spends 27 years on the island, building a home for himself, and making friends with the natives, before finally being rescued. This is the account of his shipwreck.*

In this distress, the wind still blowing very hard, one of our men early in the morning cried out, "Land!" and we had no sooner ran out of the cabin to look out, in hopes of seeing whereabouts in the world we were, but the ship struck upon a sand, and in a moment, her motion being so stopped, the sea broke over her in such a manner that we expected we should have all perished immediately; and we were immediately driven into our close quarters, to shelter us from the very foam and spray of the sea.

It is not easy for anyone, who has not been in the like condition, to describe or conceive the consternation of men in such circumstances. We knew nothing where we were, or upon what land it was we were driven, whether an island or the main, whether inhabited or not inhabited; and as the rage of the wind was still great, though rather less than at first, we could not so much as hope to have the ship hold many minutes without breaking in pieces, unless the winds, by a kind of miracle, should turn immediately about. In a word, we sat looking one upon another, and expecting death every moment, and every man acted accordingly, as preparing for another world, for there was little or nothing more for us to do in this. That which was our present comfort, and all the comfort we had, was that, contrary to our expectation, the ship did not break yet, and that the master said the wind began to abate.

Now, though we thought that the wind did a little abate, yet the ship having thus struck upon the sand, and sticking too fast for us to expect her getting off, we were in a dreadful condition indeed, and had nothing to do but to think of saving our lives as well as we could. . . . We had another boat on board, but how to get her off into the sea was a doubtful thing. However, there was no room to debate, for we fancied the ship would break in pieces every minute, and some told us she was actually actually broken already.

In this distress, the mate of our vessel lay hold of the boat, and with the help of the rest of the men, got her slung over the ship's side; and getting all into her, let go, and committed ourselves to God's mercy and the wild sea. . . .

"PULLING AS WELL AS WE COULD TOWARDS THE LAND."

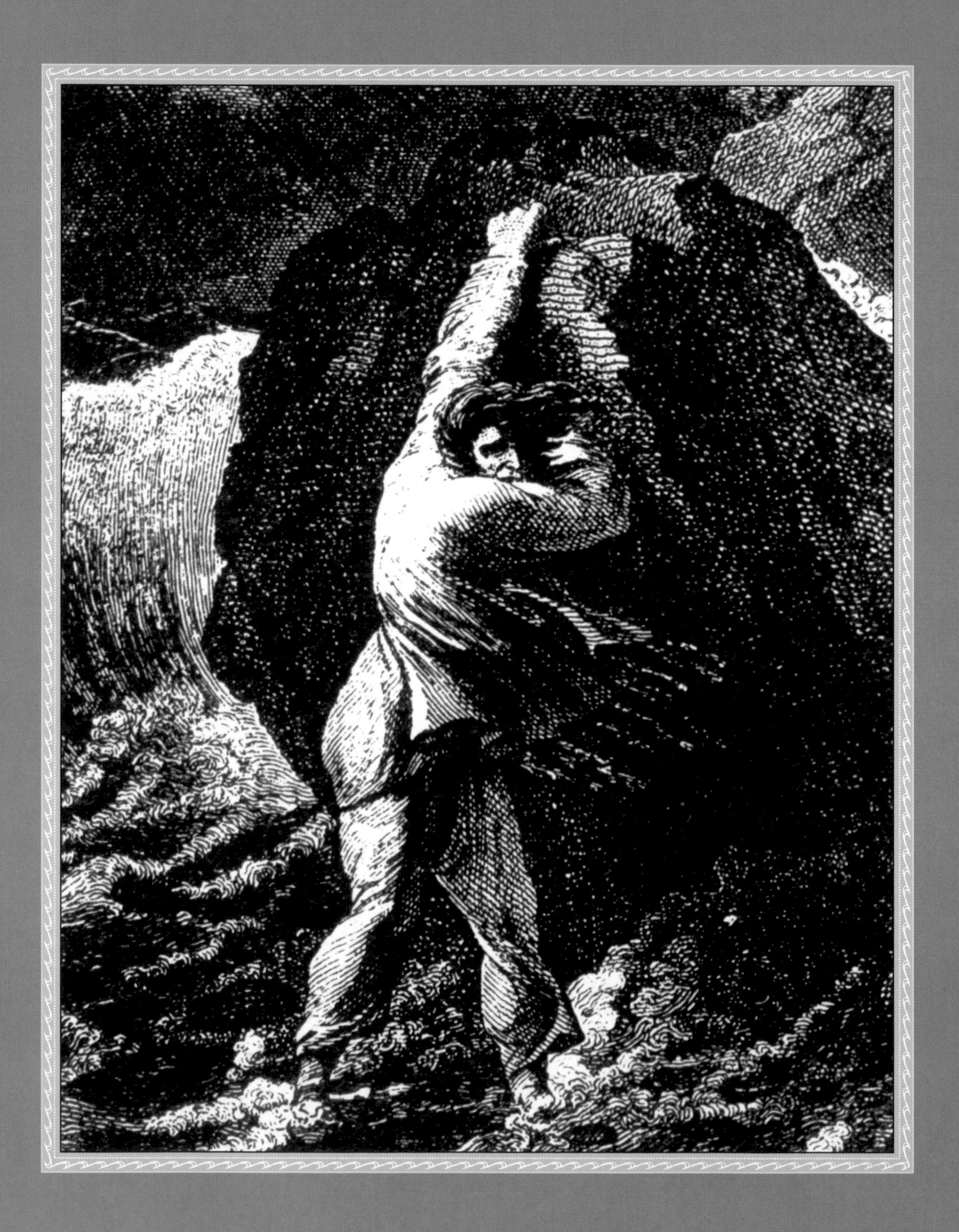

And now our case was very dismal indeed for we all saw plainly that the sea went so high that the boat could not live, and that we should be inevitably drowned. As to making sail, we had none, nor, if we had, could we have done anything with it, so we worked at the oar toward the land, though with heavy hearts, like men going to execution, for we all knew that when the boat came nearer the shore, she would be dashed in a thousand pieces by the breach of the sea. . . .

What the shore was, whether rock or sand, whether steep or shoal, we knew not. . . .

After we had rowed, or rather driven, about a league and a half, as we reckoned it, a raging wave, mountain-like, came rolling astern of us and . . . it took us with such fury that it overset the boat at once, and separated us, as well from the boat as from one another. . . .

Nothing can describe the confusion of thought that I felt when I sank into the water; for though I swam very well, yet I could not deliver myself from the waves so as to draw breath, till that wave, having driven me, or rather carried me, a vast way on toward the shore, and having spent itself, went back, and left me upon the land almost dry, but half-dead with water I took in. I had so much presence of mind, as well as breath left, that seeing myself nearer the mainland than I expected, I got upon my feet, and endeavored to make on toward it as fast as I could, before another wave should return and take me up again. . . .

But neither would this deliver me from the fury of the sea, which came pouring in after me again, and twice more I was lifted up by the waves and carried forward as before, the shore being very flat.

The last time of these two had well near been fatal to me, for the sea . . . dashed me against a piece of rock . . . with such force that it left me senseless, and indeed helpless . . . for the blow taking my side and breast, beat the breath as it were quite out of my body, and had it returned again immediately, I must have been strangled in the water. But I recovered a little before the return of the waves. Now as the waves were not so high as at first, being near land, I held my hold till the wave abated and then fetched another run, which brought me so near the shore that the next wave, though it went over me, did not carry me away. And the next run I took I got to the mainland, where, to my great comfort, I clambered up the cliffs of the shore, and sat me down upon the grass, free from danger, and quite out of the reach of the water.

I was now landed and safe on shore, and began to look up and thank God that my life was savedin a case wherein there was some minutes before scarce any room to hope. I believe it is impossible to express to the life what the ecstasies and transports of the soul are when it is so saved, as I may say, out of the very grave. . . .

I walked about on the shore, lifting up my hands, and my whole being, as I may say, wrapped up in the contemplation of my deliverance. . . reflecting upon all my comrades

that were drowned . . . for I never saw them afterward, or any sign of them, except three of their hats, one cap, and two shoes that were not fellows.

I cast my eyes to the stranded vessel, when the breach and froth of the sea being so big, I could hardly see it, it lay so far off, and considered, Lord! how was it possible that I could get on shore?

After I had solaced my mind with the comfortable part of my condition, I began to look round me, to see what kind of place I was in, and what was next to be done.

Mr. Midshipman Hornblower

(An excerpt)

BY C. S. FORESTER

During the Napoleonic wars, the navies of Britain and France fought fierce battles in the waters around France and Spain. In the exciting stories by Forester, a young man, Horatio Hornblower, begins a career in the British Navy and immediately distinguishes himself through his heroism and daring.

This excerpt is from the first book. Hornblower's ship, the Indefatigable, *joins battle with a French ship. Hornblower is stationed high at the top of the rear, or mizzen, mast, where he must try to fire downward at the French ship.*

The *Indefatigable* was slightly the faster ship; an occasional touch of the starboard helm was working her closer to the enemy, into decisive range, without allowing the Frenchman to headreach upon her. Hornblower was impressed by the silence on both sides; he had always understood that the French were likely to open fire at long range and to squander ineffectively the first carefully loaded broadside.

"When's he goin' to fire?" asked Douglas, echoing Hornblower's thoughts.

"In his own good time," piped Finch.

The gap of tossing water between the two ships was growing narrower. Hornblower swung the swivel gun round and looked along the sights. He could aim well enough at the Frenchman's quarterdeck, but it was much too long range for a bag of musket balls—in any case he dared not open fire until Pellew gave permission.

"Them's the men for us!" said Douglas, pointing to the Frenchman's mizzen top.

It looked as if there were soldiers up there, judging by the blue uniforms and the cross-belts. The French soldiers saw the gesture and shook their fists, and a young officer among them drew his sword and brandished it over his head. With the ships parallel to each other like this the French mizzen top would be Hornblower's particular objective should he decide on trying to silence the firing there instead of sweeping the quarterdeck. He gazed curiously at the men it was his duty to kill. So interested was he that the bang of a cannon took him by surprise; before he could look down the rest of the Frenchman's broadside had gone off in straggling fashion, and a moment later the *Indefatigable* lurched as all guns went off together. The wind blew the smoke forward, so that in the mizzen top they were

not troubled by it at all. Hornblower's glance showed him dead men flung about on the *Indefatigable*'s deck, dead men falling on the Frenchman's deck. Still the range was too great—very long musket shot, his eye told him.

"They're shootin' at us, sir," said Herbert.

"Let 'em," said Hornblower.

No musket fired from a heaving masthead at that range could possibly score a hit; that was obvious—so obvious that even Hornblower, madly excited as he was, could not help but be aware of it, and this certainty was apparent in his tone. It was interesting to see how the two calm words steadied the men. Down below the guns were roaring away continuously, and the ships were nearing each other fast.

"Open fire now, men!" said Hornblower. "Finch!"

He stared down the short length of the swivel gun. In the coarse V of the notch on the muzzle he could see the Frenchman's wheel, the two quartermasters standing behind it, the two officers beside it. He jerked the lanyard. A tenth of a second's delay, and then the gun roared out. The musket balls must have spread badly; only one of the helmsmen was down and someone else was already running to take his place. At that moment the whole top lurched frightfully; Hornblower felt it but he could not explain it. There was too much happening at once. The solid timbers under his feet jarred him as he stood—perhaps a shot had hit the mizzenmast. Finch was ramming in the cartridge; something struck the breech of the gun a heavy blow and left a big splash of metal there—a musket bullet from the Frenchman's mizzen top. . . . A bullet struck the barricade beside him as Hornblower trained the gun down, but he gave it no thought. Surely the top was swaying more even than the sea justified? No matter. He had a clear shot at the enemy's quarterdeck. He tugged at the lanyard. He saw men fall. He actually saw the spokes of the wheel spin round as it was left untended. Then the two ships came together with a shattering crash and his world dissolved into a chaos compared with which what had gone before was orderly.

The mast was falling. The top swung round in a dizzy arc so that only his fortunate grip on the swivel saved him from being flung out like a stone from a sling. It wheeled round. . . . The mast crashed forward: the topmast caught against the mainyard and the whole structure hung there before it could dissolve into its constituent parts. . . . With the lower end of the mast resting precariously on the deck, and the topmast resting against the mainyard, Hornblower and Finch still had a chance of life, but the ship's motion, another shot from the Frenchman, or the parting of the over-strained material could all end that chance. The mast could slip outward, the topmast could break, the butt-end of the mast could slip along the deck—they had to save themselves if they could before any one of these imminent events occurred. . . . Hornblower's eyes met Finch's; Finch and he were clinging to the swivel gun, and there was no one else in the steeply inclined top.

The starboard side mizzen topmast shrouds still survived; they, as well as the topmast, were resting across the mainyard, strained taut as fiddle strings, the mainyard tightening them just as the bridge tightens the strings of a fiddle. But along those shrouds lay the only way to safety—a sloping path from the peril of the top to the comparitive safety of the mainyard.

The mast began to slip, to roll, out toward the end of the yard. Even if the mainyard held, the mizzenmast would soon fall into the sea alongside. All about them were thunderous noises—spars smashing, ropes parting; the guns were still bellowing and everyone below seemed to be yelling and screaming.

The top lurched again, frightfully. . . . Finch's staring blue eyes rolled with the movement of the top. Later Hornblower knew that the whole period of the fall of the mast was no longer than a few seconds, but at this time it seemed as if he had at least long minutes in which to think. Like Finch's, his eyes stared round him, saw the chance of safety.

"The mainyard!" he screamed.

Finch's face bore its foolish smile. Although instinct or training kept him gripping the swivel gun he seemingly had no fear, no desire to gain the safety of the mainyard.

"Finch, you fool!" yelled Hornblower.

He locked a desperate knee round the swivel so as to free a hand with which to gesticulate, but still Finch made no move.

"Jump, damn you!" raved Hornblower. "The shrouds—the yard. Jump!"

Finch only smiled.

"Jump and get to the maintop! Oh, Christ—!" Inspiration came in the frightful moment. "The maintop! God's there, Finch! Go along to God, quick!"

Those words penetrated into Finch's addled brain. He nodded with sublime unworldliness. Then he let go of the swivel and seemed to launch himself into the air like a frog. His body fell across the mizzen topmast shrouds and he began to scramble along them. The mast rolled again, so that when Hornblower launched himself at the shrouds it was a longer jump. Only his shoulders reached the outermost shroud. He swung off, clung, nearly lost his grip, but regained it as a counterlurch of the leaning mast came to his assistance. Then he was scrambling along the shrouds, mad with panic. Here was the precious mainyard, and he threw himself across it, grappling its welcome solidity with his body, his feet feeling for the footrope. He was safe and steady on the yard just as the outward roll of the *Indefatigable* gave the balancing spars their final impetus, and the mizzen topmast parted company from the broken mizzenmast and the whole wreck fell down into the sea alongside. Hornblower shuffled along the yard, whither Finch had preceded him, to be received with rapture in the maintop by Midshipman Bracegirdle. Bracegirdle was not God, but as Hornblower leaned across the breastwork of the maintop he thought to himself that if he had not spoken about God in the maintop Finch would never have made that leap.

"Thought we'd lost you," said Bracegirdle, helping him in and thumping him on the back. "Midshipman Hornblower, our flying angel."

HOFF
Titanic
REGIE: HERBERT SELPI
SYBILLE SCHMITZ · HANS NIELSE
KIRSTEN HEIBERG · E.F. FÜRBRINGE
KARL SCHÖNBÖCK · OTTO WERNICK
CHARLOTTE THIELE · THEODOR LOO
SEPP RIST · FRANZ SCHAFHEITLI

The "Unsinkable" *Titanic*

BY WILLIAM GARZKE JR.

Titanic was a British passenger ship that struck an iceberg and sank in the North Atlantic Ocean in 1912. The disaster occurred on the liner's first voyage, from Southhampton, England, to New York City. The *Titanic* sideswiped the iceberg at about 11:40 P.M. on April 14. The impact caused a number of small cracks and failed riveted seams in the ship's hull. Seawater flooded through the bow of the ship. About 2½ hours later, the vessel broke in two and sank.

The *Titanic* carried enough lifeboats for only half of its approximately 2,200 passengers and crew. The first rescue ship to reach the site, the British liner *Carpathia*, arrived about 4 A.M. and picked up 705 survivors, most of whom were women and children. A total of 1,517 people died in the disaster. The *Titanic*'s captain, Edward J. Smith, went down with the ship. Also among the dead were many wealthy and famous passengers, including millionaire John Jacob Astor and department store owner Isidor Straus.

The *Titanic* was the largest and most luxurious ocean liner of its time. It displaced more than 52,000 long tons of water and measured 882½ feet in length. Many people believed the ship was unsinkable because its hull was divided into 16 watertight compartments. Even if 2 of those compartments flooded, the ship could still float. As the result of the collision with the iceberg, 6 compartments initially flooded.

In 1985, a team of French and American scientists led by Robert D. Ballard of the United States and Jean-Louis Michel of France found the wreckage of the *Titanic.* The ship lay in two sections about 400 miles southeast of Newfoundland at a depth of about 12,500 feet.

For years, people thought that the *Titanic* sank because the iceberg cut a huge gash in its hull. The study of steel samples from the ship concluded that the hull was made of a steel that became brittle in the frigid North Atlantic waters and fractured easily during the collision. Inquiries have also shown that the *Titanic* was traveling too fast for an area where there was danger of icebergs. The ship was traveling about 21 knots (nautical miles per hour), nearly its top speed, when lookouts sighted the deadly iceberg.

Lobster Quadrille

BY LEWIS CARROLL

"Will you walk a little faster!" said a whiting to a snail;
"There's a porpoise close behind us, and he's treading on my tail.
See how eagerly the lobsters and the turtles all advance!
They are waiting on the shingle—will you come and join the dance?
Will you, won't you, will you, won't you, will you join the dance?
Will you, won't you, will you, won't you, won't you join the dance?

"You can really have no notion how delightful it will be
When they take us up and throw us, with the lobsters, out to sea!"
But the snail replied "Too far, too far!" and gave a look askance—
Said he thanked the whiting kindly, but he would not join the dance.
Would not, could not, would not, could not, would not join the dance.
Would not, could not, would not, could not, could not join the dance.

"What matters it how far we go?" his scaly friend replied,
"There is another shore, you know, upon the other side.
The further off from England the nearer is to France—
Then turn not pale, beloved snail, but come and join the dance.
Will you, won't you, will you, won't you, will you join the dance?
Will you, won't you, will you, won't you, won't you join the dance?"

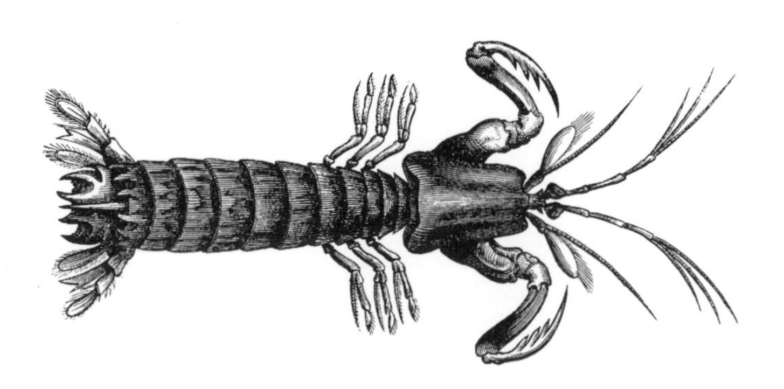

M.L.Kirk

Treasure Island

(Excerpts)

BY ROBERT LOUIS STEVENSON

Treasure Island *is the story of an expedition to recover the fabled treasure of the pirate captain Flint. On the journey is young Jim Hawkins, who narrates, Abraham Gray, Doctor Livesey, and Captain Smollett. Unbeknownst to them, however, their cook is in fact Long John Silver, a pirate and once a member of Captain Flint's pirate crew.*

Here, they have arrived at Skeleton Island, where the treasure is buried (and where one of Flint's pirates, Ben Gunn, was marooned three years ago). Long John Silver and part of the crew have mutinied and stolen the treasure map from Captain Smollett. Silver has captured Jim, but has spared his life, and takes Jim with him as they look for the buried gold.

We made a curious figure, had anyone been there to see us; all in soiled sailor clothes, and all but me armed to the teeth. Silver had two guns slung about him—one before and one behind—besides the great cutlass at his wrist, and a pistol in each pocket of his square-tailed coat. . . . I had a line about my waist, and followed obediently after the sea-cook, who held the loose end of the rope, now in his free hand, now between his powerful teeth. For all the world, I was led like a dancing bear.

The other men were variously burthened; some carrying picks and shovels . . . others laden with pork, bread, and brandy for the midday meal. . . .

Well, thus equipped, we all set out—and straggled, one after another, to the beach, where the two gigs awaited us. . . .

We pulled easily, by Silver's directions, not to weary the hands prematurely; and, after quite a long passage, landed at the mouth of the second river. . . . Thence, bending to our left, we began to ascend the slope toward the plateau. . . .

All of a sudden, out of the middle of the trees in front of us, a thin, high, trembling voice struck up the well-known air and words:

"Fifteen men on the dead man's chest—
Yo-ho-ho, and a bottle of rum!"

I have never seen men more dreadfully affected than the pirates. The color went from their six faces like enchantment; some leaped to their feet, some clawed hold of others; Morgan groveled on the ground.

"It's Flint, by—!" cried Merry. . . .

"Come," said Silver, struggling with his ashen lips to get the word out, "this won't do. Stand by to go about. This is a rum start, and I can't name the voice: but it's someone skylarking—someone that's flesh and blood and you may lay to that." . . .

George Merry was greatly relieved.

"Well, that's so," he said. "You've a head upon your shoulders, John, and no mistake. 'Bout ship, mates! This here crew is on a wrong tack, I do believe. And come to think on it, it was like Flint's voice, I grant you, but not just so clear-away like it, after all. It was liker somebody else's voice now—it was liker—"

"By the powers, Ben Gunn!" roared Silver.

"Ay, so it were," cried Morgan, springing on his knees. "Ben Gunn it were!"

"It don't make much odds, do it, now?," asked Dick. "Ben Gunn's not here in the body, any more 'n Flint."

But the older hands greeted this remark with scorn.

"Why, nobody minds Ben Gunn," cried Merry; "dead or alive, nobody minds him."

It was extraordinary how their spirits had returned, and how the natural color had revived in their faces. Soon they were chatting together, with intervals of listening; and not long after, hearing no further sound, they shouldered the tools and set forth again, Merry walking first with Silver's compass to keep them on the right line with Skeleton Island. . . .

The thought of the money as they drew nearer, swallowed up their previous terrors. Their eyes burned in their heads, their feet grew speedier and lighter, their whole soul was bound up in that fortune, that whole lifetime of extravagance and pleasure, that lay waiting there for each of them. . . .

"Huzza, mates, all together!" shouted Merry, and the foremost broke into a run.

And suddenly, not ten yards further, we beheld them stop. A low cry arose. Silver doubled his pace . . . and next moment he and I had come also to a dead halt.

Before us lay a great excavation. . . . In this were the shaft of a pick broken in two and the boards of several packing-cases strewn around. On one of these boards I saw, branded with a hot iron, the name *Walrus*—the name of Flint's ship.

All was clear to probation. The *cache* had been found and rifled: the seven hundred thousand pounds were gone! . . .

Each of these six men was as though he had been struck. But with Silver the blow passed almost instantly. . . . He kept his head, found his temper, and changed his plan before the others had had time to realize the disappointment.

"Jim," he whispered, "take that, and stand by for trouble."

And he passed me a double-barreled pistol.

At the same time he began quietly moving northward, and in a few steps had put the hollow between us two and the other five. . . .

The buccaneers, with oaths and cries, began to leap, one after another, into the pit, and to dig with their fingers. . . . Morgan found a piece of gold. . . .

"Two guineas!" roared Merry, shaking it at Silver. . . .

"Dig away, boys," said Silver, with the coolest insolence; "you'll find some pig-nuts and I shouldn't wonder." . . .

They began to scramble out of the excavation, darting furious glances behind them. . . .

Well, there we stood, two on one side, five on the other, the pit between us, and nobody screwed up high enough to offer the first blow. . . .

But just then—crack! crack! crack!—three musket-shots flashed out of the thicket. Merry tumbled head-foremost into the excavation; the man with the bandage spun round . . . and fell all his length upon his side, where he lay dead, but still twitching; and the other three turned and ran for it with all their might.

Before you could wink, Long John had fired two barrels of a pistol into the struggling Merry. . . .

At the same moment the doctor, Gray, and Benn Gunn joined us, with smoking muskets, from among the nutmeg trees. . . .

Long John, mopping his face, came slowly up with us.

"Thank ye kindly, doctor," says he. "You came in in about the nick, I guess, for me and Hawkins. And so it's you, Ben Gunn!" he added. "Well, you're a nice one, to be sure." . . .

Ben, in his long, lonely wanderings about the island, . . . had found the treasure; he had dug it up (it was the haft of his pickaxe that lay broken in the excavation); he had carried it on his back, in many weary journeys, from the foot of the tall pine to a cave he had on the two-pointed hill at the north-east angle of the island, and there it had lain stored in safety since two months before the arrival of the *Hispaniola*. . . .

As we passed the two-pointed hill, we could see the black mouth of Ben Gunn's cave, and a figure standing by it, leaning on a musket. It was the squire; and we waved a handkerchief and gave him three cheers. . . .

And thereupon we all entered the cave. It was large, airy place, with a little spring and a pool of clear water, overhung with ferns. The floor was sand. Before a big fire lay Captain Smollett; and in a far corner . . . I beheld great heaps of coin and bars of gold. That was Flint's treasure that we had come so far to seek, and that had cost already the lives of seventeen men from the *Hispaniola*. How many it had cost in the amassing, what blood and sorrow, what good ships scuttled on the deep, what brave men walking the plank blindfold,

what shot of cannon, what shame and lies and cruelty, perhaps no man alive could tell. . . .

At last, one fine morning, we weighed anchor, and stood out of North Inlet. . . .

Well, to make a long story short, we got a few hands on board, made a good cruise home, and the *Hispaniola* reached Bristol. . . . Five men only of those who had sailed returned with her. . . .

All of us had an ample share of the treasure, and used it wisely or foolishly, according to our natures. Captain Smollett is now retired from the sea. . . .

Of Silver we heard no more. . . .

Oxen and wain-ropes would not bring me back again to that accursed island; and the worst dreams that ever I have are when I hear the surf booming about its coasts, or start upright in bed, with the sharp voice of Captain Flint still ringing in my ears: "Pieces of eight! pieces of eight!"

Mary Anne

AUTHOR UNKNOWN

All day, all night, Mary Anne,
Down by the seaside, sifting sand.
All the little children love Mary Anne,
Down by the seaside, sifting sand.

The Fisherman and His Wife

BY THE BROTHERS GRIMM

A fisherman once lived contentedly with his wife in a little hut near the sea, and he went every day to throw his line into the water.

One day, after angling for a long time without even a bite, the line suddenly was pulled to the bottom, and when he pulled it up again there was a large flounder hanging to the end of it.

"Oh, dear!" exclaimed the fish; "good fisherman, let me go, I pray you; I am not a real fish, but a prince in disguise. I shall be of no use to you, for I am not good to eat. Put me back again into the water, and let me swim away."

"Ah," said the man, "you need not make yourself anxious. I would rather let a flounder who can speak swim away than keep it."

With these words, he placed the fish back in the water, and it sank away out of sight. Then the fisherman went home to his wife.

"Husband," said the wife, "have you caught anything today?"

"I caught a flounder," he replied, "who said he was an enchanted prince; so I threw him back into the water, and let him swim away."

"Did you not wish?" she asked.

"No," he said; "what would I wish for?"

"Why, at least for a better hut than this dirty place. How unlucky you did not think of it! He would have promised you whatever you asked for. Go and call him now; perhaps he will answer you still."

The husband did not like this task at all; he thought it was nonsense. However, to please his wife, he went and stood by the sea. When he saw how green and dark it looked, he felt much discouraged, but made up a rhyme and said:

"Flounder, flounder, in the sea,
Come, I pray, and talk to me;
For my wife, Dame Isabel,
Sent me here a tale to tell."

The fish came swimming up to the surface, and said, "What do you want with me?"

"Ah," said the man, "I caught you and let you go again today, without wishing; and my wife says I ought to have wished, for she cannot live any longer in such a miserable hut as ours, and she wants a better one."

"Go home," said the fish. "Your wife has all she wants."

So the husband went home, and there was his wife, no longer in her dirty hut, but sitting at the door of a neat little cottage, looking very happy.

She took her husband by the hand and said, "Come in, and see how much better it is than the old hut."

So he followed her in, and found a beautiful parlor, and a bright stove in it, a soft bed in the bedroom, and a kitchen full of earthenware, and copper vessels for cooking. Outside was a little farmyard, with hens and chickens running about, and, beyond, a garden containing plenty of fruits and vegetables.

"See," said the wife, "is it not delightful?"

"Ah, yes," replied her husband, "as long as it seems new you will be quite contented; but after that we shall see."

"Yes, we shall see," said the wife.

A fortnight passed, and the husband was quite happy, till one day his wife startled him by saying, "Husband, after all, this is only a cottage, much too small for us, and the yard and the garden cover very little ground. If the fish is really a prince in disguise, he could very well give us a larger house. I should like, above all things, to live in a large castle built of stone. Go to your fish, and ask him to build us a castle."

"Ah, wife," he said, "this cottage is good enough for us; what do we want with a castle?"

"Go along," she replied, "the flounder will be sure to give us what you ask."

"Nay, wife," said he; "the fish gave us the cottage, but if I ask again he may be angry."

"Never mind," she replied, "he can do what I wish easily, and I have no doubt he will; so go and try."

The husband rose to go with a heavy heart, and when he reached the shore the sea was quite black, and the waves rushed so furiously over the rocks that he was terrified, but again he said,

"Flounder, flounder, in the sea,
Come, I pray, and talk to me;
For my wife, Dame Isabel,
Sent me here a tale to tell."

"Now then, what do you want?" said the fish, lifting his head above the water.

"Oh dear!" said the fisherman, in a frightened tone, "my wife wants to live in a great stone castle."

"Go home," was the reply. "Your wife has all she wants."

The husband hastened home, and where the cottage had been there stood a great stone castle, and his wife tripped down the steps, saying, "Come with me, and I will show you what a beautiful dwelling we have now."

So she took him by the hand, and led him into the castle, through halls of marble, while numbers of servants stood ready to usher them through folding doors into rooms where the walls were hung with tapestries, and the furniture was of silk and gold. From these they went into other rooms equally elegant, where crystal mirrors hung on the walls, and the chairs and tables were of rosewood and marble. The soft carpets sunk beneath the footstep, and rich ornaments were arranged about the rooms.

Outside the castle was a large courtyard, in which were stables and cowsheds, horses and carriages, all of the most expensive kind. Beyond this was a beautiful garden, full of rare flowers and delicious fruit, and several acres of field and park land, in which deer, oxen, and sheep were gazing—all, indeed, that the heart could wish was here.

"Well," said the wife, "is not this beautiful?"

"Yes," replied her husband, "and you will think so as long as your mood lasts, and then, I suppose, you will want something more."

"We must think about that," she replied, and then they went to bed.

Not many mornings after this, the fisherman woke to find his wife dressed in a robe and crown. She exclaimed, "Get up, husband, and come to the window! Look here, ought you not to be king of all this land? Then I should be queen. Go tell the fish I want you to be king."

"Ah, wife," he replied, "I don't want to be king. I can't go and ask that."

"Well," she replied, "if you don't wish to be king, I wish to be queen, so go and tell the fish what I say."

"It's no use, wife; I cannot."

"Why not? Come, there's a good man, go at once; I must be queen."

The husband turned away in a sorrowful mood. He went down to the shore, but a dreadful storm had arisen, and he could scarcely stand on his feet. But still he called up the fish with the old song, and told him his wife's wish.

"Flounder, flounder, in the sea,
Come, I pray, and talk to me;
For my wife, Dame Isabel,
Sent me here a tale to tell."

"What!" cried the fish, rising to the surface, "She is still not content? Go home," said the fish. "Your wife has all she deserves."

He went home, to find all the glories and the riches vanished, and his wife sitting in the old hut, alone.

Little John Bottlejohn

BY LAURA E. RICHARDS

Little John Bottlejohn lived on the hill,
And a blithe little man was he;
And he won the heart of a little mermaid
Who lived in the deep blue sea.

And every evening she used to sit
And sing on the rocks by the sea:
"Oh, Little John Bottlejohn! Pretty
John Bottlejohn!
Won't you come out to me?"

Little John Bottlejohn heard her song,
And he opened his little door;
And he hopped and he skipped, and he
skipped and he hopped
Until he came down to the shore.

And there on a rock sat the little mermaid,
And still she was singing so free—
"Oh, Little John Bottlejohn! Pretty
John Bottlejohn!
Won't you come out to me?"

Little John Bottlejohn made a bow,
And the mermaid she made one, too,
And she said: "Oh! I never saw anything half
So perfectly sweet as you.

"In my beautiful home, 'neath the
ocean foam,
How happy we both should be!
Oh, little John Bottlejohn! Pretty
John Bottlejohn!
Won't you come down with me?"

Little John Bottlejohn said: "Oh, yes,
I'll willingly go with you;
And I never will quail at the sight of
your tail,
For perhaps I may grow one too."

So he took her hand, and left the land,
And plunged in the foaming main;
And Little John Bottlejohn, pretty
John Bottlejohn,
Never was seen again.

Little Toot

(An excerpt)

BY HARDIE GRAMATKY

That was too much for Little Toot. He wasn't wanted anywhere or by anyone.

With his spirits drooping he let the tide carry him where it willed. He was so lonesome. . . .

Floating aimlessly downstream he grew sadder and sadder until he was utterly miserable. He was sunk so deep in his own despair that he didn't even notice that the sky had grown dark and that the wind was whipping up into a real storm.

Suddenly he heard a sound that was like no sound he had ever heard before—it was the ocean. The great ocean that Little Toot had never seen. And the noise came from the waves as they dashed and pounded against the rocks.

But that wasn't all. Against the black sky climbed a brilliant, flaming rocket.

When Little Toot looked hard, he saw jammed between two huge rocks, an ocean liner which his father had towed many times up and down the river.

It was truly a terrible thing to see. . . .

Little Toot went wild with excitement! He began puffing those silly balls of smoke out of his smokestack. . . .

And as he did, a wonderful thought struck him. Why, those smoke balls could be seen 'way up the river, where his father and grandfather were. So he puffed a signal, thus. . . .

'Way up the river they saw it. . . .

Of course they had no idea who was making the signals, but they knew it meant "come quickly." So they all dropped what they were doing to race to the rescue.

Out from many wharves steamed a great fleet—big boats, fat ones, and skinny ones . . . with Big Toot himself right in the lead like an admiral at the head of his fleet . . .

Just in time, too, because Little Toot, still puffing out his S.O.S, was hard put to stay afloat.

Before he could spit the salt water out of his smokestack, still another wave came along and tossed him up again. . . .

It looked as though he'd never get down.

All this was pretty awful for a tugboat that was used to the smooth water of the river. What made it terrifying was the fact that out of the corner of his eye, when he was thus hung on a wave, Little Toot saw that the fleet wasn't able to make headway against such fierce seas.

Even Grandfather Toot was bellowing he had never seen such a storm.

Little Toot was scared green. . . .

Something had to be done. But all that Little Toot had ever learned to do was blow out those silly smoke balls.

Where he was, the channel was like a narrow bottleneck with the whole ocean trying to pour in at once.

That was why the fleet couldn't make any headway. The force of the seas simply swept them back. . . .

Indeed, they were on the verge of giving up entirely when suddenly above the storm they heard a gay, familiar toot. . . .

It was Little Toot. Not wasting his strength butting the waves as they had done. But bouncing from crest to crest, like a rubber ball. The pounding hurt like everything, but Little Toot kept right on going.

And when Big Toot looked out to sea through his binoculars, he saw the crew on the great vessel throw a line to Little Toot.

It was a wonderful thing to see. When the line was made fast, Little Toot waited for a long moment. . . .

And then, when a huge wave swept under the liner, lifting it clear of the rocks, he pulled with all of his might. The liner came free!

The people on board began to cheer. . . .

And the whole tugboat fleet insisted upon Little Toot's escorting the great boat back into the harbor.

Little Toot was a hero! And Grandfather Toot blasted the news all over the river.

Well, after that Little Toot became quite a different fellow. He even changed his tune. . . .

And it is said that he can haul as big a load as his father can . . .

. . . that is, when Big Toot hasn't a very big load to haul.

Pinocchio

(Excerpt from the Inside the Belly of the Whale passage)

BY CARLO COLLODI

Pinocchio set out gropingly in the midst of that darkness, and feeling his way along the inside of the Whale, he advanced one step at a time toward the faint light that he saw glimmering far, far off.

And as he walked, he felt his feet splashing in a pool of greasy, slippery water that gave off such an acrid smell of fried fish.

And the farther he advanced, the brighter and more distinct the glimmer of light became, until after walking and walking, he finally got to it; and when he did get to it . . . what did he find? I'll give you a thousand guesses: he found a small table laid for a meal, with a burning candle stuck in a green glass bottle on it; and sitting at the table was a little old man, all white as though he were made of snow or whipped cream, who was chewing with difficulty on some small live fishes so very alive that even while he was eating them, they would sometimes leap right out of his mouth.

At that sight poor Pinocchio was seized by such a great and unexpected joy that he practically became delirious. He wanted to laugh, he wanted to cry, he wanted to say so many, many things; but instead he mumbled indistinctly and stammered a few broken incoherent words. Finally, he succeeded in letting out a shout of joy; and opening his arms wide, he threw himself around the old man's neck and began to exclaim:

"Oh, dear, dear Father! At last I've found you again! Now I'll never leave you again, never, never again!"

"Then my eyes do not deceive me?" replied the old man, rubbing his eyes. "Then you're really my own dear Pinocchio?"

"Yes, yes, it's me, really me! And you've already forgiven me, haven't you? Oh, dear Father, how good you are! And to think that instead I . . . Oh, but if you only knew how many misfortunes have fallen on my head and how many things have gone wrong for me! Just think that on the day you sold your jacket, poor dear Father, and bought me the spelling book so that I could go to school, I ran away to see the puppets . . . and then a lie slipped from me and my nose began to grow and couldn't pass through the bedroom door anymore . . . when I came out, I saw a beautiful bunch of grapes in a field, but I got caught in an animal trap, and the peasant with all the right in the world put a dog collar on me so that I'd guard his chicken coop . . . and seeing me cry the Pigeon said to me: 'I saw your father building a little boat to go and look for you,' and I said: 'Oh, if I only had wings too!' and he said: 'Do you want to go to your father?' and I said: 'Oh, do I! But who'll take me there?' and he said: 'I'll take you to him,' and I said: 'How?' and he said: 'Climb on my back,' and so we flew all night, then in the morning all the fishermen who were looking out to sea said to me: 'There's a poor man in a boat who's drowning,' and from far away I recognized you immediately, because my heart told me it was you, and I signaled to you to come back to shore."

"I recognized you, too," said Geppetto, "and I would have been glad to get back to shore, but what could I do? The sea was rough, and a big wave overturned my boat. Then a horrible Whale who was nearby no sooner saw me in the water than he rushed toward me, stuck out his tongue, caught me up neatly, and swallowed me as if I were a tart."

"And how long have you been trapped in here?" asked Pinocchio.

"Ever since that day. It must be two years by now. Two years, my dear Pinocchio, that have seemed like two centuries to me."

"But how have you managed to survive? And where did you find the candle? And who gave you the matches to light it?"

"I'll tell you everything now. The fact is that the same storm that upset my boat also caused a merchant ship to sink. All the sailors were saved, but the ship sank to the bottom; and this same Whale, who had a splendid appetite that day, after swallowing me, also swallowed the ship."

"What? He swallowed it whole in one mouthful?" asked Pinocchio, astounded.

"All in one mouthful; and he spat out only the mainmast, because it had got stuck between his teeth like a fishbone. Quite fortunately for me, the ship was loaded not only with tins of preserved meat, but also with hardtack, that is, ship biscuits, bottles of wine, raisins, cheese, coffee, sugar, tallow candles, and boxes of wax matches. With all that bounty from heaven, I've been able to survive for two years. But now I'm down to the end; now there's nothing left in the pantry, and this candle you see lit is the last one I have left."

"And then?"

"And then, my dear boy, we'll both be left in the dark."

"Then there's no time to lose, dear Father," said Pinocchio. "We have to think about getting away right now."

"Getting away? But how?"

"By escaping through the Whale's mouth, and throwing ourselves into the sea."

"That's easy for you to say, dear Pinocchio, but I don't know how to swim."

"What does that matter? You can get astride my shoulders, and since I'm a strong swimmer, I'll bring you safe and sound to the shore."

"You're dreaming, my boy!" replied Geppetto, shaking his head and smiling sadly. "Do you think it's possible that a puppet, barely three feet tall, as you are, can have enough strength to swim with me on his shoulders?"

"Give it a try, and you'll see! In any case, if it's written in heaven that we must die, at least we'll have the great consolation of dying clasped together."

And without another word Pinocchio took the candle in his hand; and lighting the way as he went ahead, he said to his father:

"Follow me, and don't be afraid."

And thus they walked a long way, traversing the whole belly and the whole length of the Whale's body. But when they reached the point where the monster's spacious throat began, they decided to stop and take a look so as to seize the right moment for their escape.

Now you should know that because the Whale was very old and suffered from asthma and palpitations of the heart, he was obliged to sleep with his mouth open, so that when Pinocchio came to where his throat began and looked up he could see on the outside of that enormous gaping mouth quite a bit of starry sky and very bright moonlight.

"This is the right moment to escape," he whispered then, turning to his father. "The Whale is sleeping like a dormouse, the sea is calm and it's as clear as day. So follow me, dear Father, and in a little while we'll be safe."

Without further ado they climbed up the sea monster's throat. . . .

They traversed the length of his tongue and surmounted his three rows of teeth. Before taking the great leap, however, the puppet said to his father:

"Climb astride my shoulders and hold your arms around me very tight. I'll take care of the rest."

As soon as Geppetto had settled himself firmly on his son's shoulders, good Pinocchio fearlessly threw himself into the water and began swimming. The sea was as smooth as oil, the moon was shining in all its splendor, and the Whale went on sleeping so soundly that not even a cannon shot would have awakened him.

Wynken, Blynken, and Nod

BY EUGENE FIELD

Wynken, Blynken, and Nod one night
Sailed off in a wooden shoe—
Sailed on a river of crystal light,
Into a sea of dew.
"Where are you going and what do
you wish?"
The old moon asked the three.
"We have come to fish for the herring fish
That live in this beautiful sea.
Nets of silver and gold have we."
Said Wynken, Blynken, and Nod.

The old moon laughed and sang a song,
As they rocked in the wooden shoe,
And the wind that sped them all night long
Ruffled the waves of dew.
The little stars were the herring fish
That lived in that beautiful sea—
"Now cast your nets wherever you wish—
But never afraid are we."
So cried the stars to the fishermen three:
Wynken, Blynken, and Nod.

All night long their nets they threw
To the stars in the twinkling foam—
Then down from the skies came the
wooden shoe,
Bringing the fishermen home;
'Twas all so pretty a sail, it seemed
As some folks thought 'twas a dream they'd
dreamed
Of sailing the beautiful sea—
But I shall name you the fishermen three:
Wynken, Blynken, and Nod.

Wynken and Blynken are two little eyes,
And Nod is a little head.
And the wooden shoe that sailed the skies
Is a wee one's trundle bed.
So shut your eyes while mother sings
Of wonderful sights that be.
And you shall see the beautiful things
As you rock on the misty sea,
Where the old shoe rocked the
fishermen three:
Wynken, Blynken, and Nod.

Little Tee Wee

BY JOHN HEARD

Little Tee Wee,
He went to sea
In an open boat;
And while afloat
The little boat bended,
And my story's ended.

Acknowledgments

We wish to thank the following properties whose cooperation has made this unique collection possible. All care has been taken to trace ownership of these selections and to make a full acknowledgment. If any errors or omissions have occurred, they will be corrected in subsequent editions, provided notification is sent to the compiler.

Front Cover	Norman Ault, from *Dreamland Shores*, 1920.
Endpapers	Christian Schuessele and James Sommerville, *Ocean Life*, 1899.
Half-title Page	B. F. Leizalt, *John Paul Jones in Battle*, 1781.
Title Page	Courtney Allen, *Scamper Bay*, 1883.
Title Page Spot	F. M. S., from *Baby Days*, 1887.
Copyright Spot	Lisl Hummell, from *More Poems for Peter*, 1931.
Preface	Q. L., from *Baby Days*, 1887.
Contents	Anonymous, *The Footprints in the Sand*, from *Chatterbox*, 1907.
	Anonymous, from *Baby Days*, 1887.
13	Maxfield Parrish, *Lamplighter*, 1922.
14–15	John Tenniel, from *Alice Through the Looking Glass*, 1872.
16	M., *Blackbeard*, n.d.
19	Florence Harrison, from *Tennyson's Guinevere and Other Poems*, 1912.
20	Maxfield Parrish, *Arabian Seas*, 1910.
22	H. J. Ford, from *The Arabian Nights Entertainments*, 1878.
24	Anonymous scrap, n.d.
25	Anonymous postcard, circa 1930.
26	Unknown scrap, circa 1940.
27	Michael Diemner, Untitled, n.d.
28	Henry C. Pitz, from *20,000 Leagues Under the Sea*, circa 1950.
31	Edourard Riou, from *20,000 Leagues Under the Sea*, 1870.
32	Unknown scrap, n.d.
33	Millicent Sowerby, from *A Child's Garden of Verses*, 1908.
34	Winslow Homer, *The Fog Warning*, 1885.
35	Raymond Sheppard, from *The Old Man and the Sea*, 1952.
36	C. F. Tunnicliffe, from *The Old Man and the Sea*, 1952.
37	Raymond Sheppard, from *The Old Man and the Sea*, 1952.
38	C. F. Tunnicliffe, from *The Old Man and the Sea*, 1952.
39	Raymond Sheppard, from *The Old Man and the Sea*, 1952.
40	Laura Knight, *Wind and Sun*, 1913.
41	Walter Richard Sickert, *Bathers at Dieppe*, 1902.
42	Fern Bisel Peat, from *Mother Goose*, 1933.

106	Howard Pyle, *Marooned*, n.d.
108	Anonymous engraving, from *Baby Days*, 1887.
111	Montague Dawson, "How to Avoid Being Pooped" detail, n.d.
112	Movie poster for *Titanic*, 1920.
114	Unknown scrap, n.d.
115	Maria Kirk, from *Alice's Adventures in Wonderland*, n.d.
116	N. C. Wyeth, from *Treasure Island*, 1911.
118	N. C. Wyeth, from *Treasure Island*, 1911.
121	Milo Winter, from *Treasure Island*, 1915.
122	Found ephemera, circa 1900.
123	Jessie Willcox Smith, *A Child's Book of Old Verses*, 1910.
124	Corine Malvern, from *Storytime Tales*, circa 1950.
127	Corine Malvern, from *Storytime Tales*, circa 1950.
128	J. H. Mitchell, from *Babyland*, 1887.
129	Warrick Gobel, from *Book of Fairy Poetry*, 1920.
131	Hardie Gramatky, from *Little Toot,* 1939.
132	Robert Sgrilli, from *Pinocchio*, 1942.
133	Luigi E. Maria Augusta Cavalieri, from *Pinocchio*, 1924.
135	Maud and Miska Petershan, from *Pinocchio*, 1932.
136	Corrado Sarri, from *Pinocchio*, 1929
137	Primo Sinopico, from *Pinocchio*, 1946.
138	Charles Copeland, from *Pinocchio*, 1904
139	Enrico Mazzanti, from *Pinocchio*, 1931.
141	Maxfield Parish, *Wynken, Blynken, and Nod*, 1904.
142	Francis Kern, from *The Annual Mammoth Book*, 1946.
143	Mars, from *Joies d' Enfants*, circa 1880.
145	Winslow Homer, *Boy with Anchor*, 1873.
Endpapers	Christian Schuessele and James Sommerville, *Ocean Life*, 1899.
Back Cover	Anonymous, n.d.